Lainey Grayson Investigates:

A Murder Most Mysterious

CW00871784

For Lainey, Tom, Eddie and ?

Lainey Grayson

As February draws-to-an-end, so too closes the book on my latest two cases.

Solving the first one was easy. It was obvious where Miss Potter's lost bunny rabbit would be headed, what with Mr Hegarty's prize winning organic cabbage patch being just down the road. After all, rabbits do have one hundred million scent cells, giving them a sense of a smell that is eight times stronger than us humans!

Discovering who gave Catherine Turner that mushy Valentines card was a harder one to fathom, because the writer had done a good job in disguising their handwriting. The key to unlocking that mystery ended up not lying in the card at all - but rather in the envelope! The way the sender had written 27 Baker Street was what tickled my suspicions. The seven with the cross through it, while it is not the way *we* typically form the number, it is commonplace in most European countries, like Germany, and it is something that must have stuck with our classmate, Stefan Schneider, before he moved here a couple of years ago.

Tying a bow neatly around that mystery should have given me such a thrill. Cracking a challenging case always used to. But not anymore! Mind you, I had not enjoyed much of anything for the past six months.

I felt unmoved by the marvellous array of colours that carpeted Chestnut Park in the autumn. Kicking through the marmalade yellow, the plum purple and the blood red leaves did nothing for me. I didn't really enjoy trick-or-treating with Primrose at Halloween, even though we dressed up as Sherlock Holmes and Watson, like we had talked about all year. Christmas was little more than an exercise in opening wrapping paper, and I did not get that feeling of utter contentment that I usually get at midnight on New Year's Eve when drinking a mug of hot chocolate brimming with marshmallows with my Dad.

Yes, it is true that not much had made me happy over the last six months. And I knew why!

Miss Mangle

Miss Mangle was horrid. She looked revolting, like a swamp monster. Her hair was always so wet and greasy; it was as if she had emerged from the bottom of the ocean with a blob of seaweed stuck to her head. Everything about her face was little and wicked. She had tiny, black rabbit dropping eyes, a sharp witch nose and her mouth was always pursed, as if sucking on a super-sour gobstopper. And boy was she wrinkled. Her skin looked like the shell of a boiled egg after it had been given a sturdy tap with a teaspoon. But I do not judge people on their looks. It was not Miss Mangle's face that bothered me. What bothered me is that her personality was even more ghastly than the way she looked. She was rotten to the core!

Teachers are supposed to be nice. They are supposed to be kind and inspire you to do great things. My last teacher, Miss Black, was like that. She motivated me. She made me think I could do anything. *Be* anything. She really encouraged Primrose and I to set up our detective agency (L.P. Detective Agency – no case too big, no case too small). She helped us design and print posters and business cards to promote ourselves effectively. Miss Black was also the one who suggested I join her at Mensa. She helped me practice the I.Q. tests and organised my entrance exam, which of course I passed with flying colours. Miss Black is a brilliant teacher. She honed my mind until it was as keen and sharp as a new steel knife.

My current teacher was the exact opposite. Miss Mangle is as nasty and as evil a human being as you ever could meet. She is horrible, ghastly, beastly and repulsive! I hated her so much. Her regime is based on fear and intimidation and being in her class was a terrifying experience. And when that surrounds you, day in, day out, the darkness spreads into every corner of your mind, like billowing smoke fills a room.

How are you supposed to enjoy anything when you are living under a dark cloud? How could I take satisfaction in the world's many wonders when I could hear a constant ticking in my head? The ticking of a clock that was always counting down to the moment when I had to return to school. On a weekday, when the school bell rang at three, it was eighteen hours until I had to return. On a Friday afternoon it was sixty-six hours. When I woke on Christmas morn – three hundred and fifteen! In every moment of every day the clock was always ticking in my mind. TICK, TICK, TICK!

And it is not just me that thinks this way. It is everyone! Why Miss Mangle became a teacher is beyond me. The only thing she likes about children is torturing them!

I will give you an example:

It was the first day of school in September and a new boy, Simon Jenkins, was joining our class after his family recently moved into the area - an unfortunate event for poor Simon. Anyway, as well as being his first day in school, it was also Simon's birthday and his Mum had sent him into school armed with a fine chocolate fudge cake, a multipack of crisps and a bucket of jelly worms to help him celebrate the occasions with his new classmates. Poor thing - he wasn't to know.

Strangely enough, Miss Mangle was a delight on our first morning together, and she was particularly pleasant to Simon. She kept smiling at him throughout lessons, and he smiled back, eagerly awaiting the slice of sticky chocolaty goodness that time and patience would surely deliver. We all knew better. We knew that the more Miss Mangle smiled at poor Simon, the more he would suffer later. And that is exactly what happened!

It was just after we had returned to class after lunch break when it happened.

"So, Simon," Miss Mangle said, slowly and gently, "your Mummy thinks we should have a party to celebrate your birthday, does she?"

"Yes, Miss Mangle," answered Simon, sitting up as keen as a meerkat.

"And what do you think, Simon? Do you think it appropriate that we have a party to celebrate your birthday on the very first day of term, when we have so much work to do and so much to learn?"

Simon did not respond this time. He began to slump down in his chair to make himself small. He sensed the heavy atmosphere that had descended upon the room from out of nowhere.

"Simon, will you come up here?" Miss Mangle asked, beckoning to him with her long, skeletal-like finger.

The rest of us sat in silence as Simon rose from his chair and made his way over to teacher's desk.

"Stand there, Simon," said Miss Mangle, pointing down to a spot on the floor, right next to her desk. Simon stood where he was told to and looked up at the smiling face of his new teacher. It is usually nice to see people smile. It can be contagious. It makes us want to smile too. But Miss Mangle's smile was not like this at all. It was not just the fact that her teeth were as crooked as a row of Victorian chimney pots, or that they were the exact same colour as a freshly laid dog poo. It was because her smile was not really a smile. It was a menacing thing. It was as if she was frowning with her mouth.

"I'm going to blindfold you now, Simon. You see I love birthday parties and could not let this one pass without giving you a little surprise. I hope you don't mind?"

He did not have much choice. Simon was getting the surprise, whether he liked it or not!

Simon stood while Miss Mangle fetched a wide roll of thick grey duct tape from the top drawer of her desk. She scratched around at it with her bony finger to find the end. Then she pulled a length of the tape out from the roll and began to twirl it around Simon's head. Around and around and around it went, first covering his eyes, then his ears and then his mouth. Layer upon layer went on and thicker and thicker it became, until the whole roll was gone. By now, Simon's entire head was covered, apart from a small slit for his left nostril, which he could breathe out of.

Miss Mangle turned to her desk and picked up her remote control. She pressed the big red button, which activated a winch on the wall at the side of the classroom. The winch slowly turned, which lowered the rope that ran up the wall and along the ceiling. Attached to the end of the rope was a box that was covered in a dusty old blanket. When the box reached head height, Miss Mangle released the red button and guided the box gently onto the desk. She then untied the rope at top of the box, before stroking it lovingly.

"Don't worry, children, you'll all soon have a chance to find what is in this box as the year progresses," she said, looking up and glancing across the sea of anxious eyes before her.

Kneeling, Miss Mangle then began to tie the loose rope around Simon's trembling ankles, twisting it together to form a fancy looking knot that looked like the numeral eight. She seemed very skilled at this - like she had tied up many things before. Miss Mangle gave the rope a firm yank to tighten the knot and stood back upright. She looked around the class and once again grinned that beastly grin before pressing the green button on the controller. This time the winch turned anti-clockwise and the rope began to rise slowly into the air. It gradually ascended to the point where it took Simon's feet clean off the ground, sending him flying onto his back with a thud. The rope continued to rise higher and higher, until eventually, Simon was hanging completely upside down in mid-air, like a prize catch fish.

"Now, Simon, on the timetable for this afternoon was Geography, but as your twit of a mother thinks that having a party is more important, we'll combine the two. You know what they do for parties in Mexico, don't you, Simon?" said Miss Mangle, as Simon swung gently from left to right.

Simon mumbled something that sounded a bit like, "Please let me down?"

Miss Mangle heard what she wanted to hear.

"Yes, that's right, Simon," she continued, "in Mexico they celebrate a party by having a piñata. They stuff an ornament full of sweets and treats and beat it repeatedly, until it breaks and all the candy tumbles to the floor."

Miss Mangle then began stuffing Simon's pockets full of crisps and jellies. She then plunged her jagged hands straight into the heart of Simon's cake, before placing giant, gooey fistfuls of the stuff down his jumper. Once she had finished, she produced two foam javelins from under her desk, that she must have plucked from the P.E cupboard earlier in the day.

"Right children - form two rows!"

Without speaking a word, we arranged ourselves into two perfectly straight lines. We then took it in turns to beat Simon, in order to release the sweets and cake pieces onto the floor. We did not want to do it. It hurt us as much as it hurt Simon. Now, when I say hurt, of course this did not hurt any of us physically, Miss Mangle never hurt anyone physically, but mentally we all took a battering that day. And that was worse! A bruise on your arm or leg will heal, in time, but a mark on your soul is a much harder thing to rid yourself of.

Once the floor was carpeted in sweets and crisp and cake crumbs, Miss Mangle let Simon down. She then peeled off all the duct tape from his head, being careful not to rip off too much of his hair from his head or eyebrows.

"Right children, you may eat now."

Miss Mangle took a seat at her desk and took great delight in watching us all eat squashed jellies and crisp and cake crumbs from an old dusty floor. None of us wanted to. But we all did. We had been downgraded to mere animals. We were like pigs, snouts down in the mud. It was utterly humiliating. And it was a quite ridiculous thing to behold.

And that is the reason why Miss Mangle got away with it.

Imagine that this had happened to you today in school. What would happen if you went home and told your parents about it? I bet that they would not believe you in a million years.

But even if they did harbour suspicions, like Simon's Mum did, that would not get you anywhere with Miss Mangle.

The following day, Simon's Mum stormed into school. She burst into the classroom first thing in the morning as we were taking our seats and demanded answers. But Miss Mangle was as cool as a cucumber. After Simon's Mum accused her of torturing her son, Miss Mangle laughed right into her face. Then she lined up all the children and said that she was going to ask us if what Simon had said was the truth. We all desperately wanted to say that it was. Primrose and I kept glancing at each other to summon up the courage to back Simon up, to expose Miss Mangle for the despicable human being that she was. But a chain is only as strong as its weakest link. Miss Mangle purposefully plucked the weakest, meekest, most feeble pupils from the line for the answers - Linda Bell, Sophie Smith and Paul Higgins. All of them said that Simon was lying.

I don't blame them. Picking a fight with a monster is a terrifying thing. So that was that! Simon's Mum went off embarrassed and furious at her son for concocting such a 'tall tale'.

After that, no other child ever spoke out. We, as a class, had an understating that this was the way it was going to be for the year. We just had to tough it out, keep our heads down and get through. But all of us hated Miss Mangle. Every one of us hated her with every fibre of our being. But did any of us really hate her enough to murder her?

The Day it all Happened

The day in school had started like any other; with us children sat in absolute silence and backs perfectly straight, displaying impeccable posture, like group of uppity schoolgirls at finishing school.

It was half past ten and we had just finished copying out Latin sentences from the board. I realise that Latin is a subject that has not been on any school curriculum for many a year, but Miss Mangle deemed it important, so we did it. Miss Mangle had her own curriculum going on. She taught what she liked, and heaven help any school inspector who came in and said she had to do things differently!

As we sat awaiting further instruction, Miss Mangle rose from her chair. Placing both hands behind her back, she made her way to the front of her desk, ready to address her prey.

"Bruce Bunter, stand up!"

Bruce flew up from his chair like a firecracker had gone off in his trousers.

"What is four multiplied by five?"

"Twenty, Miss," said Bruce.

It was the correct answer. This disappointed Miss Mangle greatly. Her little dark eyes darted across the room.

"Grace Smith, stand."

Grace bolted up like a jack in the box.

"What is seven times six?"

"Forty-two, Miss," said Grace. And although she knew the answer like the back of her hand, you could still hear a wobble in her voice. You see, she knew what would happen if she got the answer wrong. It is funny what happens under intense pressure. Even things you think you know for sure you can become uncertain of. Even a simple question like, 'what is your name?' could flummox someone under ultra-stressful conditions.

Once again, Miss Mangle looked around the room, more slowly this time.

All eyes were fixed on her. You see, over time, we had learned that if you avoided her gaze, she would know that you didn't know, so you needed to look confident, even if you had no idea of the answer to the question. But I didn't need to pretend. I knew all my times tables. I had known them since I was six. I don't want to sound big headed, but I knew all the answers to every one of Miss Mangle's questions. Miss Mangle hated me for knowing everything. It meant that she couldn't punish me as much as some of the others. And because I knew all the answers, she rarely asked me. She only asked me something every now and again in the hope I may not have been listening - something that happened early in the year, but something I vowed I would never let happen again.

Miss Mangle gazed right at me. A cold shiver shot down my spine. She hovered over me for a second, but eventually I was bypassed. Her head creaked to the left and her gaze fixed upon Jimmy Cotton. Jimmy looked at Miss Mangle. He had the steely glare of a professional poker player. But he did not fool her. She knew he was going to struggle with the upcoming questions. He always did. It wasn't fair. It wasn't his fault. He had tried to learn his tables, but, as in most areas of school life, Jimmy struggled.

"Jimmy," she said slowly and dangerously, "what is five times eight?"

I could see Jimmy's fingers fidgeting behind his back, as he desperately tried to count up in fives."

"It's forty, Miss," he said.

"Very good, Jimmy," she said sarcastically. "Aren't you a clever boy?" It was like she was talking to a pet puppy rather than an eleven-year-old boy. "Right, Jimmy, we are on a roll here, so let us continue. What are six sixes?

Again, Jimmy used his fingers, took his time and said, "Thirty-six."

"Good, Jimmy," she said. And then, as quick as a flash, she barked, "Seven eights!"

Jimmy was not at all confident in his sevens, and he certainly didn't know his eights. I knew it, Jimmy knew it and most certainly, Miss Mangle knew it.

After a long period of silence, Jimmy answered, "Fifty-nine, Miss?"

"Fifty-nine is it?" she paused. "Jimmy, will you come up here."

Jimmy slowly walked up to the front of the class, before reluctantly taking Miss Mangle's vacated chair, behind her desk. We all knew the drill by now. The minute Jimmy sat down, Miss Mangle pressed the red button on her controller that turned the wheel at the side of the room, which lowered the rope that held the box. Jimmy didn't even look up. It was best not to. In only a few seconds the box hovered just a few inches above Jimmy's head. Miss Mangle then yanked off the cloth that covered it, like a magician whipping a tablecloth from under a stack of glasses. And so was revealed her pride and joy – a box containing a huge clutter of spiders!

The box was clear plastic. There was a hatch at the top, for which to put in new spiders, and a larger hole - the exact size of the average fifth grader's head - at the bottom. The hole was covered in a thin layer of rubber, with a small pin-prick hole in the centre. It was small enough that no spiders could escape but, when forced, the hole could stretch open just enough to allow a child's head inside.

By now the box had fully descended and we could see the outline of Jimmy's face all squashed and squished and deformed as it wrestled its way through the rubber. And then Jimmy's head popped free, into the tank.

We had all made a pact, that no matter what, we would not act scared - no matter what. We wouldn't give her the satisfaction. Besides, you couldn't scream in the tank anyway - spiders would just crawl into your mouth. But while Jimmy was trying to be courageous, I briefly caught a glimpse of the panic in his eyes before his face was swallowed by the swarm of spiders.

There were so many spiders in the tank that it was hard to tell one from the other. From our chairs it just looked like black smoke. But we knew every species that were in there. We knew because Miss Mangle told us regularly. There were hundreds, if not thousands, of normal house spiders and daddy-long-legs, which lived side by side with more exotic varieties. There were huntsman spiders, wolf spiders, orb spiders, peacock spiders, sparklemuffins and even a skeletorus. But there was one spider in there that we all feared the most – Goliath! Goliath was a tarantula. A Brazilian whiteknee tarantula to be precise. A big beast of a thing it was. From its thick muscular torso protruded eight meaty legs. Legs even hairier than Miss Mangle's!

I felt for Jimmy. I myself had been in the tank twice. Once in September, when I was daydreaming about a case and Miss Mangle asked me a question and again in November, when I accidently forgot to complete one sum for homework. That was nearly four months ago now, but I remember as clear as day the feeling of Goliath's strong legs crawling across my forehead. It was like a giant's furry hand drumming its fingers on my face.

By now we had counted to ten.

"Eleven, twelve, thirteen, fourteen."

Miss Mangle made the class count to the correct answer to help the recently mistaken child 'learn it.' And it did help to a degree. Everyone in the class knew ten times ten. No one wanted to have their head in that tank for one hundred seconds!

And then, suddenly, the door opened and in walked William Wiggins, a cup of hot tea in a bone china cup in one hand and a saucer piled high with custard creams in the other. I could see his knuckles were white as he held onto the items for dear life. Spilling something would, of course, spell trouble. William carefully crossed the classroom and placed the items down delicately on the desk of Miss Mangle.

"Forty-nine, fifty, fifty-one, fifty-two."

Once we had reached the correct answer of fifty-six, Miss Mangle pressed the green button, and the box began slowly lifting from Jimmy's head. Eventually, Jimmy's head burst free, and Miss Mangle re-covered the box with the blanket to hide the spiders' existence from any parent or teacher that ever dared enter the room - not that anyone ever did! The box continued to rise upwards until it settled back at the top of the ceiling.

Jimmy, meanwhile, was trying to look unfazed by the whole ordeal, but I could see he was a few shades paler than he was before he went in and his fringe was plastered to his forehead with terror sweat.

Miss Mangle looked at Jimmy and smiled, displaying her set of putrid gnashers. "Will you remember that now, Jimmy?"

"Yes, Miss." he said.

As Jimmy returned to the desk, Miss Mangle whipped round and turned her attention to William. "What way was this tea stirred, William?"

"Clockwise, Miss."

Miss Mangle always knew which way the tea had been stirred. I know that sounds crazy, but it is true. She knew. You could put one hundred cups of tea in front of her, half stirred clockwise and half anti-clockwise and she would know, one hundred times out of hundred, which was which.

Now, most teachers have a cup of tea and a chat with their colleagues at break-time, but Miss Mangle was not one for socialising. It was clear as day that the other teachers hated her as much as we did. Not that that would bother her. So instead, five minutes before break-time, one of us children had to go to the staff room to make her tea and fetch her seven custard creams. The tea bag had to be in the water for exactly forty-five seconds before being removed. And then the tea had to be stirred ten times clockwise. Not too fast and not too slow.

Miss Mangle slowly raised the cup to her mouth, her eyes unmoving from William. The rim of the cup reached her paper-thin liver lips, and she slurped a mouthful of the liquid back into her throat. Even the way she drank tea was horrible. She sounded like a vacuum cleaner that had accidentally taken up a sock.

"And this was stirred ten times was it?" asked Miss Mangle.

William nodded. "Yes, Miss Mangle."

With that, the bell went. But no one moved a muscle. Miss Mangle took one more sip as she continued to stare at William. She appeared satisfied.

"Right, get out of here the lot of you and leave me in peace," she barked.

We did not need telling twice. We got up and headed outside. Little did we know at the time that that was the last time we would ever see Miss Mangle alive again!

Break-time

Primrose and I sat, cross legged, on the bank while the chaos of the playground swarmed around us. Children were whirling, twirling and running in all directions. A huge game of soccer toed and froed in the middle of the field, with a rabble of angry looking children crowded around a tired looking ball, kicking it to pieces. Shrill screams punctuated the air. It was louder and more boisterous than normal. But then, it was very gusty. I had observed on numerous occasions that the pupils' behaviour in school was always more rambunctious when the wind picked up. It had happened way too often to be co-incidence. But it never affected Primrose and I. Whatever the weather, we always sat calmly and chatted at break-time, usually discussing the intricacies of cases.

So, are we going to take it on?" asked Primrose, eagerly.

"I don't know. It's not the most exciting or glamorous case," I replied.

"Come on, Lainey. I know it's not the greatest case in the world, but it's still another chance to see your brilliant mind at work."

Primrose always flattered me. It wasn't the primary reason that I called her my best friend, but I have to admit, it didn't hurt.

It is funny that Primrose was named Primrose. A girl called Primrose you would expect to have gorgeous strawberry, blonde hair, wear beautiful flowery dresses, smell of sweet perfume and have a cherubic face sprinkled with freckles, like a dusting of icing sugar on a pancake. My Primrose was nothing like this. She was gothic. She had long, straight, jet-black hair and, outside of school, she wore baggy black jumpers and tight black jeans that moved down to clunky black boots. Had it been a long weekend or a school holiday her fingers would have been coated in black nail varnish too, and her lips smothered in black lipstick. In fact, if it were not for her piercing green eyes and porcelain white skin, she would most certainly be completely invisible in the dark.

"Okay, let's go and check out the crime scene then," I said, rising to my feet.

Someone had been setting off stink bombs in the girls' toilet at break time, which had led to many girls grumbling and moaning to me about it. Solving the case surely would not prove much of a challenge. My Moriarty would be far more sophisticated than to be using stink bombs. But I suppose it was still important to take on, and solve, every case that came my way. I needed as much practice as possible if I was going to be the world's most famous detective when I was older. That has been my ambition ever since I can remember. It all stemmed from my Grand dad, whose favourite television show was Columbo, a detective that graced the screens back in the sixties. With a glass eye, scruffy bird's nest hair and a cheap tan mackintosh, he didn't look like a genius. But his mind was brilliant! If you had committed a murder and he was on the case, you would undoubtedly be put away for it sooner or later. I used to love nothing better than sitting watching Columbo with my Grandad. Curled up on that battered but - oh-so-comfy - sofa with the fire crackling, slurping cola from the can while Columbo set about proving the culprit's guilt gave me a feeling of contentment that I will never forget, and it is what ultimately set me off on my love of solving crimes.

Primrose and I wandered across the warzone of a playground until we eventually reached Mr Marston who was bent over chatting to a sprout of a child. It was Sally from junior infants. Two long streams of luminous green snot hung from her nose, dangling dangerously close to her mouth.

"Excuse me, Mr Marston, can we go to the bathroom please?" asked Primrose.

Mr Marston looked up. He seemed happy to end his conversation with snotty Sally.

"Both of you need the toilet at the same time is it?" he probed.

"Yes," said Primrose, I need a wee and Lainey needs a poo."

"Primrose," I whispered through gritted teeth and giving her a small jab into her ribs to boot.

"Go on then," chuckled Mr Marston.

I knew he would let us go. He is another one of the nice teachers - almost as nice as Miss Black. He is the sixth-class teacher at the minute, and I hope that he would stay there and teach us next year; it would be a welcome break from Miss Mangle. Mind you, being taught by a savage Rottweiler would be an improvement on her.

Primrose and I continued across the playground, counting backwards from ten down to one as we hopped the hopscotch in reverse. We navigated the child on the floor holding a badly grazed knee and waded through the concerned rabble of well-wishers, over to the double doors that led inside. Just as we were about to walk in, William Wiggins bolted out. He looked like he was in a mighty rush.

And as soon as we entered the main corridor the smell hit me. It was the stench of rotten eggs. It was ghastly. Someone had set off another stink bomb! Primrose and I pinched our noses tightly as we began making our way down the corridor.

"Hello, Mrs Goggins," we said, as we passed the school secretary, our pinched noses making it sound as if we had the flu.

"Morning, girls," she said, smiling through the stench.

As we neared the girls' toilets, Primrose pulled her phone from her pocket with her spare hand. We were not actually allowed phones in school, but Primrose always had hers with her in case we needed to document anything for one of our cases and she regularly took photos and videos for evidence. She was caught one time by Miss Mangle, which of course led to the box of spiders being placed on her head, but Primrose, strangely enough, was the only one in the class who did not seem to care a jot about being in that torture chamber.

We slowed our pace and quietened our steps as we approached our classroom. We were allowed to use the toilet at break time, but we still didn't want Miss Mangle to see us as we passed. The less she saw you the less chance there was of her making trouble for you. As we tip-toed along I glanced through the small square window of the classroom door to see if she was looking. And that is when I saw her.

Ding Dong, the Witch is Dead!

Miss Mangle was hunched over. Her head was down, and her face covered by her mop of slimy wet hair that spread across the desk like a pot of spilled ink. Her arms were also flopped on top of the desk and I knew instantly that something was wrong.

"Primrose, look," I said, stopping dead in my tracks.

Primrose moved closer to the window and peered through. She did not say anything. Instinctively she turned the handle and walked into the room. I followed close behind. As we approached, I feared the worst. Primrose was more optimistic. "Maybe she's asleep," she said, secretly knowing, as I did, that Miss Mangle was dead!

You would think that being in the presence of a dead body would scare a child. That it would freak them out or send a cold shiver down their spine. But I did not feel any of these things. I wasn't nervous, shocked or overawed. On the contrary - I felt wildly alive. My brain was on fire, popping like corn kernels in a hot saucepan. You see, there was something strange about Miss Mangle's body. Something unnatural. There was something just not right! I imagined what Columbo would think if he were here. And this thought was thrilling to me.

Primrose was on the same page and instantly whipped out her phone and set about taking photos.

As I studied Miss Mangle's body in more detail, things became even more compelling. Her left hand was giving a thumbs up sign, and in her right, she held a black biro, with the letter W roughly scrawled on a piece of lined paper in front of her.

I was absorbed by it all. I felt like a sponge soaking up all the information around me, as it if were liquid. I was utterly transfixed on the potential crime scene before me.

The spell was broken the minute Miss Black appeared from round the corner and hurtled into the room.

"My goodness, what's happened?" she said.

"It's Miss Mangle. I think something has happened to her," Primrose replied. "I think she's... dead!"

Miss Black ran toward the desk and brushed us aside. "Stay back, girls," she said as she approached Miss Mangle. Miss Black proceeded to press two of her well-manicured fingers onto the neck of Miss Mangle and rubbed them around, presumably to find a pulse.

"Girl's, go and get help," she said, looking up. "Go and get the other teachers."

Miss Black then began caressing the cheek of Miss Mangle, rubbing her hand up and down the side of her face. "It is okay, my dear, you're at peace now."

Meanwhile, Primrose and I remained rooted to the spot. We had heard Miss Black tell us to go and raise the alarm, but we seemed completely incapable of moving.

"Girl's please, you need to go and get help now! And Primrose, turn off the phone. It is really not appropriate to be taking photos of this."

Of course, Miss Black was right. But Primrose was not being morbid or being disrespectful to the dead, it was just her habit. Her phone was always clicking away when we smelled something fishy going on. But Primrose heeded Miss Black's words and placed her phone back into her pocket.

Miss Black on the other hand had just pulled hers out from her designer handbag and had begun dialing for an ambulance.

Meanwhile, Primrose and I had finally sprung into life. We dashed out of the room and down the corridor toward the staff room.

We knocked on the door but burst in before waiting for an invitation to enter.

As the door swung open, we were greeted by a sea of teacher eyes. They clearly wondered what on Earth could be so important as to disturb their precious coffee break.

"Come quick," said Primrose, "Miss Mangle is dead."

The teachers just sat there gawping at us. It seems that while the human brain takes around thirteen milliseconds to process information normally, obviously big news, such as this, takes longer to sink in. Mr Large's mouth was the first thing to move. It dropped opened, revealing a half-chewed tuna sandwich. Eventually Mrs Rogers rose to her feet, and then, one by one, all the other teachers began hoisting themselves up from their chairs and shuffling out into the corridor.

"I'll go and get Mr Williams," said Mrs Rogers as she walked in the opposite direction to everyone else. She looked extremely pale. While she may have been trying to be useful, I suspect she was trying to avoid seeing a corpse.

When we reached the classroom, Miss Black was stood by the door, which she had shut behind her. "I'm afraid poor Miss Mangle has passed," she said. "The ambulance is on its way. There's nothing to do now but wait."

The Police Roll into Town

By now, many of the pupils had gone home. A message had gone out to all the parents informing them that the school was shutting due to an emergency and that they should collect their children as quickly as possible. However, Primrose and I were still on the scene, for once hoping that we could stay in school as-long-as possible. As we sat on the top step, just before the entrance door, a police car arrived, siren blaring. It drove up and parked neatly behind the ambulance. The siren ceased, the door slowly opened, and PC Herman rolled out onto the pavement. And when I say rolled out, I mean *rolled* out, for PC Herman was as round an individual as you were ever likely to meet. A perfectly spherical man, his navy-blue uniform stretched over his skin like taught balloon, making him look like a giant blueberry. PC Herman hustled and bustled past the parents and children as if they were not there, although, when he reached the top step and saw us, he stopped briefly and nodded his head. You see PC Herman knew me well. I was always hanging round the police station asking the officers questions to help me become a better detective. I had even asked to do work experience there during the summer holidays, but I was too young. Only another four years, three months and seventeen days until I was able to get a taste of the action - not that I am counting or anything!

PC Herman then turned and shook the principal's hand furiously. "Right will you escort me to the scene," he said gruffly. PC Herman's bushy moustache covered the entirety of his mouth, so when he talked, you couldn't see his lips move, just the swaying of the hairs above his upper lip that looked like a caterpillar enjoying a zumba class.

Mr Williams, the school principal, escorted PC Herman inside the building. Poor Mr Williams. He was always such a jolly fellow but today he looked a shadow of his normal self. He was visibly shaken and completey drained of colour, like a vampire had sucked all the blood from his body.

I was surprised to see PC Herman return to the front of the building after only a few minutes of being inside. He was scribbling notes furiously in his notepad with a tiny pencil. I had always wondered where police officers get those miniature pencils. The only place I have ever seen them is in Argos. But PC Herman couldn't have stolen it from there though, could he?

Despite being busy taking notes, I was desperate to find out some information of my own. "So what tests are you doing, PC Herman?" I asked eagerly. "Fingerprints and DNA profiling for starters, I assume?"

PC Herman shook his basketball sized head. His wiry moustache bristled into life. "They'll be no tests, Lainey. It's as clear as day that Miss Mangle died of natural causes."

"But what about her thumb sticking up, don't you think that's a bit weird?"

"Lainey, the woman was eighty-one years old!"

Primrose and I looked at each other. Eighty-one years old! No wonder she looked ancient- she was ancient! She was probably already able to draw a pension during the moon landing. An eighty-one-year-old teacher must be some sort of world record. I was not even sure that it was legal. Don't teachers have to retire in their sixties?

"And what's more," continued PC Herman, "she had a bad heart. She had to take a large cocktail of strong tablets every day, from what I hear. Most likely the poor woman had a heart attack. No, there is no mystery to solve here. She was a poor old woman that died of natural causes and I've given the paramedics permission to take her to the hospital."

"But what about the W she had written on the paper?"

"P.C Herman removed his eyes from his notebook and fixed them squarely on me. "What about it?" he said sternly. "She was probably just writing something when it happened. Look, in this line of work I have had the dis-pleasure to see many a dead body and many of them are in strange positions. It was only a few months ago I found a man sat on the toilet with his eyes wide open reading a newspaper. He was like a waxwork in Madame Tussauds." PC Herman paused for a moment. "Lainey, I shouldn't even be talking about this with you. You are eleven years old. Go and solve your little mysteries about missing pets and stolen garden gnomes and leave the grown-up stuff to me." PC Herman then sighed an enormous sigh and shook his head as if he were cross at himself for getting cross at me. "Look, one day you'll make a fine detective. I am sure of that. But in this instance, I want this to be the end of it."

My Thoughts Racing

But that wasn't the end of it. I couldn't sleep that night. I lay in bed watching the shadows of the branches of the apple tree outside move and sway across my ceiling. Usually that relaxes me - but not tonight. I could not stop thinking about Miss Mangle. But my thoughts weren't those of sadness, as you would typically imagine when someone you know dies, it was more confusion, mixed with a rather large dose of curiosity. Despite her age and her bad heart and what PC Herman had said about bodies often being in unusual positions, something still felt wrong. Firstly, and I know that this may sound stupid, but she just wouldn't have died in school. She wouldn't have given any of us the satisfaction of seeing her in a moment of weakness. I know that sounds daft. People cannot choose the moment a heart attack strikes or the moment they die. It just happens. But I knew that Miss Mangle could.

Her thumb sticking up. Why?

And why did she write the letter W? Granted, she may have begun to write something and had a heart attack mid-way through, but what was she writing? And more importantly why was she writing it in black? I am surprised she even owned a black pen. It was always red with her. She loved putting big red crosses in the pupils' books with her red biros.

Plus, everyone had a motive. The whole school hated her. The whole town did. Even the hairs on her head hated her, so it wouldn't come as a huge surprise if she had driven someone to murder.

By the time I reached Primrose's house at half past eight the following morning I was exhausted. I felt like my mind had run a marathon. But I summoned the energy to knock on the door and was welcomed in by Primrose's mother, who instantly began offering tea and toast. I accepted. I had learned it was best to just take what was on offer from Primrose's Mum, or else the offers would never cease.

Primrose's Mum was the opposite of Primrose. She was plump and soft and warm and all smiles. A lovely giant marshmallow was what she was. "Terrible what happened yesterday, wasn't it?" said Mrs Edwards from the kitchen. I could hear her loudly scraping butter across the toast as I sat on the sofa in the front room. "It's only right you all got the day off today to recover from it."

School was shut today. It was deemed appropriate we all had time to mourn, although it is terrible to say this, but no-one was sad.

"Yes, it was a tragedy," I replied. Both Primrose's Mum and I felt not a jot of sadness about Miss Mangle's death but we, like everyone else, would keep up the pretense.

Mrs Edwards strode into the room and thrust a plate of buttered toast into my hand. "There you go dear, eat up," she beamed.

It was only toast, but the happiness she took in feeding people made it feel like she had just handed me a precious ingot of gold. "I'll go and get Primrose up. She'd lie in all day if I didn't wake her."

I began munching through the buttered toast while listening to footsteps and muffled conversations upstairs. The toast was far too buttered for my liking. Deep puddles of yellow scummy liquid floated on the surface and if the toast was not perfectly level it began running down my fingers like hot wax dripping down a candle. But saying that to Primrose's Mum would crush her like an empty soda can being stood on, so I ate up. I had nearly finished by the time Primrose dragged herself down the stairs in her black onesie and threw herself in a heap upon the sofa.

"William Wiggins," I said, before she even had a chance to fully open her eyes.

"What about him?" Primrose yawned.

"I've been going over it all night and the pieces of the puzzle suggest that he could have killed Miss Mangle."

To identify and catch a killer they must meet three criteria.

First, they must have an opportunity to do the crime, which means they must be in the area at the time and have no alibi – evidence that they were somewhere else, or were with someone else, when the crime was committed.

"Remember, we saw William racing out of the building just before we found Miss Mangle dead. And I was thinking, he was the one who made her the tea yesterday and his Dad is a pharmacist. It wouldn't be hard for him to snatch something deadly and slip it into her cuppa."

This is the second thing a detective needs to know – the means. You need to know how the killer committed the crime.

"And what about the motive?" asked Primrose, still sceptical.

A motive is the third corner of the murder triangle. It is the reason someone has for committing the crime. This is a bit of a problem in this case because everyone had a motive. Past pupils wanted revenge, present pupils wanted rid, and fourth graders dreaded having her next year. And all the teachers plain hated her. But William may have a little stronger motive than most.

"United played on Monday night, didn't they?"

"And?" said Primrose.

"And the last time they played on a school night, William came in the next day and he hadn't done his homework because he had watched the match with his Dad and forgot to do it."

"Oh yeah, I remember that. William's head was in the tank for half an hour that day." she said, chuckling to herself, even though it was an absolutely horrid thing.

"And do you remember what Miss Mangle said after he was released?"

I continued, before waiting for Primrose's response.

"She said that if he ever did it again, she would make him eat a football. Do you think she was joking about that?"

"Miss Mangle never joked," said Primrose.

Well then if he didn't do his homework then he must have been awfully scared. That is a strong motive for murder.

Primrose shook her head. "I'm sorry but I cannot believe that William killed Miss Mangle. It's preposterous!"

"But what about the W that Miss Mangle had written on the piece of paper? I was thinking – what if she was beginning to write William, to let the police know he has poisoned her, but died before she could finish?"

"Lainey, he's eleven. And he is a right wimp. He cried like a baby a few weeks ago when he missed a penalty in the soccer match against Holy Trinity. He's not a murderer."

"Perhaps not," I said, "but you are letting outside influences cloud your judgement. Remember what I have told you before - you must forget what you *think* you know and follow the breadcrumbs, no matter which unlikely direction they may lead. And I think that if Miss Mangle was murdered then William, at this moment in time, is the most likely culprit."

Primrose nodded as if she agreed but I knew it was just to humour me. She was a good assistant.

"So, what are we going to do about it?" she asked.

"Well, for starters, we need to get into school and check out the classroom. I want to see if William's homework is in the pile, and I also want to get a sample of the tea that Miss Mangle was drinking. If his homework is not there and we prove there is something nasty in the tea, we'll have him bang to rights! I just hope that they haven't completely cleared the classroom yet and removed the evidence."

"But school is shut today. We won't be able to get in," replied Primrose, who had now fully awakened.

"It's shut for the pupils but maybe the teachers had to go in? But if not, we could try and pick the lock - you know I have been practicing. It's worth a shot."

Suddenly, like a ghost, Primrose's Mum appeared from seemingly out of thin air.

"What are you girls up to?" she asked suspiciously.

"Nothing," replied Primrose, "We were just planning to head out for a bit and make the most of our day off."

"Okay, my love," said Mrs Edwards "You go and get changed then and I'll put on some more toast. I'll make it extra buttery for you this time, Lainey – just the way you like it."

Gathering Evidence

Visiting a school without any children is an odd experience. On a normal day, the noise and the laughter and the chaos makes the place feels alive and vibrant. Take that way and you are left with nothing more than a cold, grey building. A cold, grey building with a blue saloon parked outside!

"That's Mr Wallace's car," said Primrose. "So, the school is open. But how are we going to get into our classroom and get the evidence without him noticing?"

"He'll probably be in his office, so he won't even know we've gone in," I said. "And I don't need to be in there long. It'll only take a minute to check on whether William's homework is in the pile and then I'll quickly get a sample of the tea that Miss Mangle was drinking," I said, rattling an empty soda bottle in front of Primrose. "So, I was thinking that while I do that you could stand outside Mr Wallace's office, so that if he happens to come out into the corridor for some reason you can keep him occupied while I get what we need."

"But what will I say to him? How will I explain why I am in school?"

Primrose looked at me, waiting for a suitable answer.

"You'll think of something," I said.

Primrose rolled her emerald eyes and sighed, sounding exasperated. But she was not fooling me. I knew that she loved navigating the often-bizarre twists and turns we would take while solving cases.

Primrose was silent as we began creeping up towards the school. I could see she was thinking of how best to explain her presence in school to Mr Wallace, should she need to, so I did not disturb her.

We did not want to go straight across the playground and be spotted by Mr Wallace from his office window before we even had a chance to look inside, so instead we hopped over the side wall and shimmied along the red bricks of the main building, before creeping silently up the steps to the front door. Gently, I pulled the door a fraction open and pressed my eye to the crack. I scanned the corridor. Empty reception area, all classroom and toilet doors closed. No-one around!

"Right, I'll head to the classroom. You head down to Mr Wallace's office and I'll meet behind the big tree on the field in ten minutes."

"Okay," said Primrose. "But you owe me for this one, Lainey."

I pushed open the front door and tiptoed quickly and quietly toward our classroom, while Primrose continued padding softly down the corridor.

When I entered the room, it felt different. Lighter somehow. Airier. It was as if the room had doubled in size since the ominous, looming presence of the foul old lady had evaporated. I felt a little bit bad every time I thought something negative about Miss Mangle or every time, I felt relief or even a pinch of happiness about her death. But in all honesty, that was the way it was.

I immediately made my way over to the pile of homework files and began thumbing through them to check if William's was there. I kept count as I flicked through them, checking the names as I went. Twelve, thirteen, fourteen. Jane Seymour, Stephen Tierney, Tim Tiddle. Eighteen, nineteen, twenty. Gary McKenna, Luke Summers, Emily Stevens. Eventually I came to the final three folders. Primrose Edwards, Jimmy Cotton and Robert Corneil. Twenty-seven in total. As I suspected, one folder missing - William Wiggins'!

I had no time to pat myself on the back though. At once I made my way over to Miss Mangle's desk. A swell of excitement tingled through my body as I reached it because I could see that it was untouched since yesterday. The W written in black biro on the page of paper still lay on the table and her cup of tea was still there! I picked up the handle and tilted it a small bit sideways to look inside. Miss Mangle had not drunk much of it. There were still around two thirds of the cup left, or at the very least - five ninths. If the tea was tampered with, the poison must have been strong and fast acting. With great care I slowly tipped some of the liquid into my empty bottle, being careful not to spill any, leaving enough as to not alert anyone to the fact I had been in the room and taken some, should they check. I screwed the top onto the bottle and checked the clock on the wall. It had taken me around four minutes to complete my mission. Plenty of time left to quietly make my escape and meet Primrose at our rendezvous point. I was just about to do this very thing, when all-of-a-sudden, the handle of the door began to turn.

Quickly I shot under the desk, curling myself up into a ball. Who was it? Hopefully, Primrose. I really did not want it to be Mr Wallace. More alarming to me though was the idea that it could be the murderer coming back to tidy up incriminating evidence at the scene of the crime, which is a highly common phenomenon, especially among disorganised killers. I sat motionless under the desk and heard the clip-clop of pointed shoes enter the room.

"Lainey, you can come out now. I know you are there. I just saw Primrose hanging around outside Mr Wallace's office and she wouldn't be here unless she was acting on your instructions."

I clambered out from under the desk and stood up.

Rumbled

"Miss Black, what are you doing here? I didn't see your car out front."

"I got a lift in with Mr Wallace to keep him company. He is really shaken up by the whole thing, so I said I would help him organise a new substitute teacher and to arrange Miss Mangle's funeral. But let's not talk about me will we - let's talk about you. Lainey, what are you up to?"

Miss Black tucked her long, perfectly straight blonde hair behind her shell-like ears and looked at me with those crystal-clear blue eyes of hers, waiting for a suitable response.

I stood there feeling fragile and vulnerable. What was I to do? What was I to say? My brain was firing on all cylinders, trying to think up an excuse. But, after a little thought, I knew I had no option other than to tell the truth. After all, Miss Black was highly intelligent. My IQ had been measured at 136 when I had been accepted into Mensa, and at the time, I had asked Miss Black hers. She never told me. However, I did suspect that it could have been even higher than mine! I am not the easiest child to teach. I know that. I always have a thousand questions. Most teachers don't know them, Google them, or usually just ignore them (Miss Mangle I never asked) but Miss Black always knew every answer to every question I ever threw her way. She was amazing. Therefore, I knew that any lie I told would shine as brightly to her as a candle flame flickering through a window on a dark winter night.

"I am looking for evidence."

"Evidence?" Miss Black asked quizzically. "You surely don't think there has been some foul play, do you? Lainey, I realise some aspects of the whole thing may seem strange to you, but it was just one of those things. Miss Mangle was old and very unwell - she died of natural causes."

"But what about the...

"Lainey, do you really think Miss Mangle was killed? And by someone in the school? Do you know the chances of being murdered?"

"Yes, it's one in sixteen thousand. But that is a worldwide statistic, including countries where murders are much more commonplace than here, so it would be a great deal less than that, but then that doesn't mean it didn't happen."

Miss Black looked at me funny. Should I not have known that?

"Lainey, the woman was eighty-one and had a bad heart and it happened in the middle of the day in a busy school. I know she was unpopular, but murder? Who would have done it? How would they have done it?"

Hearing PC Herman say she died of natural causes was one thing but hearing it from Miss Black was harder. She was usually right - about everything! Maybe I was reading too much into the clues. But then I had come this far, I had to at least finish what I had started. The bottle containing the tea was on the floor by my feet and as I stood in front of Miss Black, I knew I had to get it without her noticing.

"Oh look, it's Primrose," I said.

The very second that Miss Black's head swiveled round, I crouched down, grabbed the bottle and stuffed it down the back of my trousers, between the bottom of my back and the waistband of my trousers, where it sat nestled snuggly.

Miss Black turned back.

"Primrose isn't there," she said, suspiciously. She began looking me up and down.

"Sorry, I thought I saw her through the window of the door. I guess I'm still a bit on edge since yesterday."

"That's understandable," said Miss Black, in a voice that sounded like she clearly knew I was up to something. "Lainey, you should go home and relax, and I'll see you tomorrow. I will not mention this to anyone if you promise that this is the end of all this."

"I promise," I said.

I didn't like lying to Miss Black.

Assembly

The next day we were back at school. But instead of heading straight to class, as was usually the way, all the children had been brought into the hall for a special assembly. It was a few minutes until nine o' clock and Mr Wallace was getting ready to address the pupils. As he sat there, in the centre of the row of teachers, I could see his hands trembling as his eyes moved across a piece of paper, presumably containing some of the things he wished to say about the whole Miss Mangle situation. Despite being as smart and well-groomed as usual, he looked nervous. But then I suppose this was not a situation that many principals found themselves in.

While most of the seats in the hall were now taken, there was still no sign of William Wiggins. If he was to be absent today, then my suspicions about him would increase ten-fold. But as the clock on the wall of the hall inched closer and closer to nine, I finally saw him enter the hall from the double doors at the back of the room. I watched him like a hawk as he walked down the aisle, scanning across each row for a vacant chair. Despite the seriousness of the situation, I could not help but always feel a little amused whenever I saw William. He was a funny looking lad. Like many other people in the world, William looked like an animal.

Many people look like a bird of some kind - an owl being the most common. People with upturned noses have a piggy quality and often people say their owners look like their dogs. But William looked like a more unusual animal – a giraffe!

By now, William had reached my row. He peered down it and caught my gazing eye, before quickly looking away. Did he look away quicker than normal? Was he avoiding my gaze? William eventually found a chair on my row, but on the opposite side of the hall.

It is a strange phenomenon when you are being watched - you can always sense it. That strange tingling sensation you get, and then, when you look up, there is someone staring right at you. William must have felt this at this precise moment because he raised his head and looked across the row at me. I quickly looked away, to try not to alert him to the fact I was watching him. But when it happened again, and then again, it must have been clear to William that I had my eye on him. He began to squirm around in his chair like a worm on a hook. Perhaps his discomfort about me watching him was the reason that his behaviour seemed strange to me? Every little thing he did was magnified in my mind. For example, why was he blinking so much? On average people blink twelve times per minute, but in the last ten seconds William had had blinked four times, and if you multiply that by six that would be twenty-four times in sixty seconds. Highly shifty!

I swept my fringe from my eyes as I continued to observe my suspect. It was annoying me. I usually had it cut exactly two centimetres above my eye line, so as not to hinder my view of any clues. A small thing really, but those small things can lead to finding big pieces of evidence that can crack a case wide open. However, it was now inching down a little too far for my liking, something I would rectify with the kitchen scissors the minute I got home.

By now, all the pupils were in the hall. Mr Wallace had stood up from his chair and had moved to the front of the stage. He raised his right hand. We pupils followed suit, a sign that we had seen him and needed to finish our conversations and hush ourselves. The chatter reduced until only a few pockets of noise remained. Then, there was silence.

"Thank you, children," said Mr Wallace. "Girls and boys, teachers, this is, this is a sad day. A day of great sadness, girls and boys. It is all very sad. It has been a shock. Very sad."

Mr Wallace was all over the place. Normally he was so happy and energetic and confident but today he was a bag of nerves as he fumbled the words in his mouth like hot chips. Mr Wallace stopped talking. His Adam's apple pulsed up and down in his neck as if swallowing great mouthfuls of liquid. He stood silent in front of us, just swallowing.

Sit down and relax, Martin, I'll do this, I lip-read Mrs Sidebottom, the vice-principal, say." Mr Wallace ambled back to his chair, sat down and stared into space.

Miss Sidebottom took the baton. She was a formidable woman. Obviously nowhere near in the same league as Miss Mangle, but she was next in line. She had developed somewhat of a thick skin and a cold, hard exterior as her teaching career progressed – she had to with a surname like Sidebottom. Children can be cruel, and she had been the butt of many jokes over the years.

"Girls and boys, teachers, the last few days have been very sad, emotional and trying for us all," she pronounced confidently, displaying to poor Mr Wallace how a speech should be delivered. "Mrs Mangle was an outstanding teacher and a dear friend, and we will all miss her terribly. But it is time to move forward now, while keeping and cherishing in our hearts the fond memories we had of her."

Fond memories? I would wager that we couldn't find one among the bunch of us.

"The school has contacted your parents to inform them that we have a councillor ready, should any of you need to talk about this. Please do not suffer alone.

Feel free to approach any staff member at any time about what happened."

Miss Sidebottom paused for a moment.

"Now, Miss Mangle's funeral is arranged for next Wednesday and if anyone would like to attend then you are very welcome. We are hiring a bus to transport staff and pupils, and more details about this will be given in due course. And finally, before we finish our assembly the school choir is going to sing a song in respect and memory of our beloved Miss Mangle."

The choir were all seated at the front of the hall. Primrose was among them. She loved singing and had a wonderful voice. And even though gospel hymns were not really her cup of tea, she took every chance she could to practice and improve her vocal technique. While she enjoyed our detective work, her career of choice was being the lead singer of a famous rock band, so being in the school choir was a must.

A hush descended. The choir began to sing. The conductor, Mrs Blake, began waving her arms around like windmills, to kick the song into top gear. Most sang adequately. A few voices were nice. Primrose's shone through the brightest of them all. She looked angelic up there. The choral shrill of a nightingale gently escaped her lips as she sang. And it was a beautiful song. Soft and pleasant and little bit melancholy, but hopeful and inspiring, too. Who knows what Primrose thought of it though? It was a far cry from the heavy metal thrashing and screaming of her favourite band - the Severed Heads - that Primrose listened to in the confines of her dungeonesque bedroom. As the song drew-to-a-close a misty-eyed Miss Sidebottom stood once more.

"Beautiful," she said wiping a tear from her eye. "Miss Mangle would have loved that."

She wouldn't!

"Now for the pupils in class five, for the remainder of the year we have a substitute teacher starting on Monday. It is Miss Candy, who I believe has taught you before. But for today and tomorrow, Miss Mangle's class will be divided up between the other classes. If you all stay behind at the end, we will inform you where you are going."

William Wiggins

Unfortunately, William and I had not been placed together. I was with Mr Marston in sixth, William was down with the infants, so I had not had any further opportunity to gauge his behaviour. But now it was break time and Primrose (who was in third) and I had been reunited in the yard. I now needed to take the fifteen-to-twenty-minute window (depending on how long the teacher's cuppa took to drink) to confront William with my suspicions and see if he would drink the tea I had collected yesterday. If he did not drink it, then we would have our culprit. Usually, it would be easy enough to locate him - star striker of the soccer team, he played in the match every day, without fail, but today he was nowhere to been seen. This was highly unusual. He must have known that I was onto him!

Primrose and I made our way over to the left-hand side of the playground and scrabbled up the grass bank. It was the highest point in the yard and gave us the best vantage point. We scanned the area. Primrose from left to right, and me from right to left, until we met in the middle. But nothing. William was no-where to be seen.

But suddenly Primrose burst into life. "Target located," she said.

"Where is he?" I asked.

"Over there," said Primrose, pointing to the sensory garden.

Standing behind the big lavender bush, I did not see him at first, but his shoes gave him away. They were hard to miss –being coloured toxic waste yellow with streaks of fluorescent pink running down the sides. They were the same soccer boots his favourite footballer wore. Long gone are the days when all the players had black ones. Unfortunate for William really, as black boots would have been much harder to spot.

"He's hiding. That is highly suspicious," I said.

Primrose narrowed her eyes and nodded. She was dubious of William's involvement at first, but I could sense that she was beginning to come around to the possibility now.

We made our way over to the sensory garden. There were two access points - under the arch covered in creeping ivy on the left, or through the wooden gate on the right. We would take one each, so that William could not escape. Primrose braved the football match and waded through the sea of players toward to arch. Meanwhile, I went around the hopscotch and silently lifted the latch on the gate. And there we met at the lavender bush. I placed up a finger, then two and then three.

"Hello, William!" I said, as we poked our heads around opposite ends of the bush.

William jumped out of his skin.

"Hi...Lainey. Primrose. How's it going?" he stuttered and spluttered.

"Don't hi me," I said. "Why aren't you playing soccer? You always play soccer."

"I'm injured. I pulled my hamstring," he said, as the idiot began rubbing his calf muscle. "So, I was just relaxing here for break time, to rest it."

"What utter tosh. You're avoiding us and you know it," I declared.

William began shuffling nervously from left to right, like he was trying to polish the floor with his bum.

Primrose took a softer approach. We had the good cop, bad cop thing off to a tee now. Despite being as hard as nails, Primrose usually took the role of the good cop. While it was a stretch to say that I did not like, or get on with, most people, it was true to say that most people found me to be rather blunt and prickly. People warmed to Primrose much easier, so she proved a much better good cop than me. When she would flutter those long black eyelashes and act all sweet and sugary, people would usually happily give up the information, after I had beaten them down first, of course.

"Leave him alone, Lainey." Her butterfly wings began to flap. "It's such a shame you're missing out on the soccer match, William. I love watching you play. You're so good."

William blushed from head to toe.

"Yeah, I'm pretty good alright," he mumbled, modestly.

"Pretty good? You're amazing!" said Primrose. "Better than Messaldo, I reckon."

William's face was so red hot now it was a wonder that the lavender bush behind him had not burst into flames.

And now, while William's guard was down, I jumped back in with the bad cop routine, hitting him with my suspicions. And I did not hold back. "So, William, you made Miss Mangle her tea yesterday, didn't you? And your dad is a pharmacist and works with potentially deadly drugs, and then you were seen running from the school building at break time. So, what I think is this - you poisoned Miss Mangle's tea and then you went in to check she had drunk it and when you saw her dead, you ran out of the building to escape the scene of the crime. Does that sound about right?"

William went from red to white in the blink of an eye.

"What are you talking about? I didn't kill her. I wouldn't do that. Why would I?"

"Well, you did hate her."

"So did you. We all did."

"But William, I know you had more reason that most. You see, when I checked the homework folders, I noticed that yours was not there. You hadn't done your homework on the day it happened. And if Miss Mangle found out, you'd be done for."

"So what if I didn't do my homework? That doesn't prove anything," sniffled whimpering William.

"Well, it gives you a strong motive, and you had the opportunity, and now, with you hiding here, surely you can see how it all looks."

"I'm only hiding because you were looking at me the whole time in assembly. I knew you were after me," said William, his voice all croaky from nerves.

"And why would I be after you, William? Because you murdered our teacher?"

"No," said William, "because I thought you were onto me about the stink bombs."

Of course. William could very well be the guilty party in the stink bomb case. It would make sense. But it could also very well be a red herring. He could have been setting off stink bombs in the girl's toilet to cover his tracks and distract us from the fact that he killed our teacher!

"That doesn't mean that you didn't poison Miss Mangle's tea though, William."

William was all in a tizzy now.

And it was back to Primrose.

"Don't worry, William," said Primrose, calmly. "If you didn't do it then there is nothing to worry about. And there is an easy way to prove to us that you had nothing to do with all this horrid murder business."

"What is it?" said William, "I'll do whatever I need to do. I've done nothing wrong."

I whipped the bottle out from my trouser pocket and shook it in front of William.

"Drink the tea, William," I said.

"The tea?" he said.

"This is the tea from Miss Mangle's cup at the time she died. I strongly suspect there is poison in there, most likely arsenic - that is the most common poison, after all. But if you drink some of it then we'll know it hasn't been tampered with and you'll be off the hook."

William shook his head wildly back and forth. "I'm not drinking that. No way!"

"As I suspected," I said, "the tea is laced with poisoned."

"It's not," protested William.

"So why not have a sip," I said, thrusting out the bottle in his direction once more.

"Because it's cold," he said. "And because...she drank out of it! There is probably some of her horrible spit in there. Her breath stank like a badger's bottom. There's no way I'm putting any of that in my gob."

"William was right - it was disgusting. I would not have drunk any of that tea for a million quid, but I needed him to drink it if he were to be ruled out. I gave Primrose the eyes.

She fiddled around in her pocket. Suddenly the faint sound of a siren drifted through the air.

"Oh dear, that's the police coming to arrest you. I warned you this would happen," I said. "They'll put you away for sure. You will be locked up in juvenile detention for days, maybe weeks, until you get bail. That is if they let you out at all. In a serious case such as this you may be banged up until your trial. And that could be months away!"

"Juvenile detention? Trial? I don't want to do any of that," whimpered William, tears welling in his eyes.

William was in luck. There were no police officers coming for him. We had used this technique on a previous case - when we suspected Sean King was stealing people's lunches from their bags. We downloaded a police siren noise onto Primrose's phone and used it to rattle him and make him think that the police were coming to arrest him. It worked a treat. We got him singing like a songbird. He was happy to confess everything if we would call off the police and he could face the lesser charge of detention. We broke him and we would break William, too. He was teetering on the edge; he just needed one more push.

"Come on, William," said Primrose, "you could be a professional soccer player one day. Why waste your talent rotting in jail."

I held out the bottle.

William grabbed it, unscrewed the lid and pinched his nose mighty hard. And then he did it. He threw back his head and took a great glug from the bottle. And then he took another and another and kept gulping until the whole lot was gone!

William lowered the bottle from his lips. He was as green as goblin now. His face had been more colours than a packet of skittles by this point.

"See, I didn't do it," he said, dribble seeping out from the cracks at the corners of his mouth. William then began to puff out his cheeks in an exaggerated fashion, as if he were about to get sick.

"No vomiting, William," I demanded. "If you puke and the tea comes out then it proves nothing."

Suddenly, Primrose threw her hand over William's mouth, and I slapped my hand over hers. And then we sat in silence for a while, hoping and praying that William would keep the tea down and not chuck up all over our hands.

Despite the gravity of the situation, it was lovely to be sat in the sensory garden. A gorgeous gentle scent seeped out from the lavender bush, despite it not being in season, and the wind chimes that hung from the weeping willow in the corner of the garden made a haunting melody as they tumbled into each other. But the peace and tranquility of it all was broken by a clip-clopping that sounded a lot like a horse trotting into the garden. I knew the sound well - it was Miss Black, the teacher on yard duty. The high heels of her posh,

Gucci shoes meant you could always hear her coming a mile away. And then, the clip-clopping ceased.

"And what is going on here, may I ask?" said Miss Black, poking her head around the corner.

"Nothing, Miss," said Primrose.

"Is William alright there?" she said, looking down at the sweaty green boy with tears in his eyes and our two hands still clamped over his chops.

"William was worried that a bee from the lavender bush may fly into his mouth, so we are protecting him," said Primrose.

This excuse would not have worked on a stupid teacher, let alone Miss Black.

"That's strange that William would be worried about that. You don't see many bees in February and it's also a bit odd that William would sit next to a bush that attracts bees if he was so scared of them. So, I will ask again, are you alright, William?"

Primrose and I moved our hands up and down, which caused William's head to nod.

"And if could you please release your hands from over William's mouth and let me hear it from himself that would be splendid, girls."

"We slowly released our hands and hoped beyond hope an explosion of vomit wouldn't burst free.

"I'm fine, Miss." said William, still looking awfully queasy.

"Right then, don't worry about those silly bees," said Miss Black smiling, her lovely ice white teeth sparkling in the winter sun. "Why don't you go off now and play football with your friends."

William did not need telling twice. He sprang to his feet and quickly made his escape.

"Now, girls," said Miss Black, "I'd wager that this has something to do with a case you are working on. I really hope that it is not something to do with Miss Mangle's death."

"Not death, Miss. Murder!" I stated. "I was certain William had done it and I was just testing out my theory but…"

Miss Black raised a finger to her lips. She sighed and shook her head. "Lainey there really is no crime to solve here. You are barking up the wrong tree. Now this is an upsetting and disturbing time for everyone in school. Having you poking around, asking questions and grilling poor students is only making it worse. Seriously, this must be the end of it all."

Maybe, Miss Black was right. After all, William had tasted the tea and lived to tell the tale. So, if he was the killer, then he must have killed Miss Mangle by a different method. Or perhaps it was not him at all? But I had been certain that it was him. This case was *so* frustrating. And solving it would undoubtedly be my hardest test to date.

Back to the Drawing Board

My eyes were streaming. Staring at a computer screen for a long period of time will do that to you. Primrose had e-mailed me the photos she had taken yesterday, and I had been at my desk looking at them on my laptop for hours. Ruling William out, or at least greatly reducing the possibility of his involvement, had brought me back to the drawing board, so I was studying every inch of every photo in the hope of finding a clue. But so far - nothing. The more I looked at it, the stranger it seemed, and I was still convinced of foul play. Miss Mangle's thumb up and the W written in black ink – it was like she was telling us something, I was certain of it, but for the life of me I could not figure out what it was. It was like she was speaking to me in a foreign language. I squeezed my eyes shut. They hurt. I reached into the top drawer of my desk for my Rubix cube and began twisting and turning it around and around, again and again. Have you ever tried to remember something - someone's name for example, but just could not recall it, but then the minute you stop trying to think about it, it just pops into your head out of the blue? It is because trying too hard to think of something puts stress on the brain and can narrow the channels in which information is retrieved. It is a bit like when there is a block in a sink and the water cannot escape. But when we relax and let our mind drift onto other things, the channels can open, and information can flow once more.

It is the same with my cases. Sometimes I find that I am thinking so hard about them, that it becomes impossible to see the wood from the trees. And that is when I take a break. It helps if I focus my mind elsewhere. Sudoku, crosswords and mindfulness colouring have all been useful in the past. The Rubix cube was my current distraction of choice. I was getting very skilled at it now. The first thing you need to do is make a daisy pattern - a yellow sticker in the middle with four white stickers surrounding it at the sides, so that it looks like a daisy. I will not bore you with the rest of the instructions to complete the cube, but if you follow a set sequence, then no matter which of the 43.2 quintillion possible combinations the cube is set in, you can solve it in twenty moves or less. And after five flicks of the wrist, I already had seven of the nine white pieces on one side nestled together. I really enjoy the Rubix cube. There is something very satisfying about seeing all the squares of the same colour come together.

The same colour squares!

I dropped my Rubix cube. My attention shot straight back to the computer. My focus narrowed. And there it was. Sat there in broad daylight the whole time - a clue!

That was why her thumb was up. Miss Mangle was pointing to the ceiling. In our school the whole roof is composed of ceiling tiles. Square pieces of foam held in place and secured into a metal grid frame. It is quite common in old schools, like ours. But upon close examination, one of the squares, the one next to the hook for the rope holding the box of spiders, was a tiny bit darker than the others. Hardly noticeable really and something you would never have seen in a million years, had you not been really looking. But I had been really looking, and I had now noticed it. Now, the obvious reason for the tile to be a little darker than the others is because it had recently been turned. You see, over time, the ceiling tiles fade very slightly from exposure to UV rays from sunlight, whereas on the opposite side, where it is dark, they are preserved. So, at some point, that particular ceiling tile had recently been turned over. Maybe the murderer was up there looking down at their victim and maybe when they replaced the tile, they put it back the wrong way? So many possibilities, so many new avenues to explore. How thrilling. The game was afoot!

What next?

After discussing this new piece of evidence with Primrose, we decided that we needed to make a list of things to do in order to crack this case. The first job was to find possible suspects. We were back to having the whole school as possible perpetrators, but we would now try and focus on finding out exactly who was in the school building during break time, paying particular attention to those who were by themselves, as they would have the best opportunity to commit the crime. We already knew that all the staff were present, excluding Mr Marston who was on duty in the yard, but were there any other children besides William who entered the building at play time? And let us not discount William Wiggins either, because while he did not poison Miss Mangle's tea, he still had a strong motive and was near the classroom at the time. And that leads us onto another vitally important job. We needed to find out what had happened to Miss Mangle. How did she die? There were no obvious signs of foul play, which is why I suspected she died of internal damage. But my suspicions about poisoned tea had evaporated with William still alive and kicking. So how did the culprit do it? Maybe it had something to do with the W that Miss Mangle had written on the piece of paper? Maybe it was not a name at all. Maybe she was telling us the method of murder - another clue that needed to be solved. I was hoping that re-examining the scene may prove useful. Maybe there would be something on the floor by the replaced ceiling tile or something up in the crawl space between the ceiling tiles and the roof that would shed some light on it?

The weekend was the longest ever. Time is a funny thing, how it can slow and quicken. I know that sounds daft, an hour is always sixty minutes, a day always twenty-four hours, but sometimes time can fly and other times it drags. Before, when I was taught by Miss Mangle, I would try and hold on to every precious second of free time, as I hated going back, but the weekends would whizz by in the blink of an eye. But this weekend, when I was itching to get back to business, time seemed to stand still.

But eventually, Monday morning did arrive.

Before school started that day, we had headed straight into Mr Marston's classroom and, while he was busy shuffling around papers and trying to organise the morning's work, we had asked him outright who had asked him to go to the toilet during yard time on the day Miss Mangle died. He was pretty-sure that William was the only one to have asked him, besides us. Not conclusive proof that no-one else was in the building. Another pupil could easily have entered without asking permission. So, we set about interviewing our next eyewitness.

Mrs Goggins was our school receptionist. She was lovely old lady who gave away smiles for free but was as useless as a paper umbrella. Important messages would be lost or mistranslated on a daily basis, and you would never in a million years dream of handing her any money for school trips or cake sales or what not. That was always given to the class teacher, or to Mr Wallace. Because Mrs Goggins was as dithery as a baffled bluebottle, I had not placed much hope on her being able to help us, but we had to give it a shot. You see, Miss Goggin's reception area was positioned right at the entrance of the school and she had a clear view the whole way down the main corridor. So, if anyone had been up to something then she would be the best person to shed some light on it.

"Morning, Miss Goggins," Primrose chirped, upon approaching her desk.

"Good Morning, Painey and Limrose. How lovely to see you both. What can I do for you?" she said, placing her cup down on top of some important looking papers and spilling a good volume of tea all over them to boot.

"Could we ask you some questions please, Miss Goggins?" I said, pulling out my notebook and pen from my trouser pocket.

"Certainly, my dear," she said, beaming from ear to ear like a Cheshire cat.

"It's about the day of the." I paused. "The day that poor Miss Mangle died."

"My goodness," said Mrs Goggins, for once not smiling but nibbling her lip instead. "A terrible business. It's a day I'll never forget as long as I live."

"That's great," said Primrose enthusiastically. "So, can you tell us all the people that you saw in the corridor that day?"

"I have absolutely no idea," said Mrs Goggins, smiling again. "I couldn't tell you. Sorry, girls."

I knew interviewing Mrs Goggins would prove problematic.

I was about to grill her a bit harder, when all of sudden, the phone rang. Mrs Goggins picked it up and answered the call, beaming from ear to ear as if she was being told she had won the lottery, rather than the fact the Harry Kingsley had a vomiting bug and had been up all-night puking all over the bed covers. As she nodded her head to Harry's mother on the other end of the phone, she waved at us, politely bidding us farewell, while she continued with her daily business.

Primrose and I left deflated. We had not narrowed down our search of suspects at all. It could still really be anyone. At this point I think we needed to change tack. Maybe focusing our attention on the ceiling tile would give us more joy.

The Ceiling Tile

Today was our first day back together in our classroom. It felt strange being back in there, minus Miss Mangle. But a good strange. We were all happy with our new teacher. Miss Candy was sweet. We had her last year when Miss Black had the flu, just after Christmas. She had not been into us this year because Miss Mangle never got sick. I'd say a virus couldn't stand being inside her foul body and would either escape at the first opportunity or just wither and die. You would probably find a cure for all manner of illnesses if she had donated her body to medical science. But that is something she would never have cared to do. Not if it benefitted others.

The class seemed to be enjoying Miss Candy's new and exciting teaching methods. The whiteboard had been turned on for the first time in forever and a fun maths game was being played. But I was not paying attention. I just sat, eyes glued to the ceiling tile, wondering about all the possibilities of why it had been flipped over, and by whom? Presumably, someone was up in the crawl space between the ceiling tiles and the concrete roof, but how would someone get up there? An adult could just about reach the tiles with their fingertips if standing on a chair or table, but only someone fit and able could jump up and pull themselves up using the metal frame that held in the tiles. That ruled out a few of the staff at least. Mr Large for one! With a breakfast roll in each hand as he entered the school gates and a lunchbox the size of a family's two-week getaway suitcase that brimmed with copious rounds of sandwiches and crisps and buns and goodness knows what other unhealthy treats for break time, he could barely tie his own shoelaces, let alone get up to, and crawl around, the tight confined crawl space. He would have taken the whole ceiling down! He was my teacher in third and could barely move. It was like being taught by one of the rocks at Stonehenge.

The more I sat there and pondered the possibilities, the more agitated I became to have a look for myself. Maybe the killer had left some clue up there that would crack this case wide open.

I needed to get up there!

Finally, it was break time and time to put my plan into action. Mr Marston was on duty again today. It was supposed to be Miss Mangle on Mondays, so it was Miss Candy's turn now, but Mr Marston, being the nice guy that he is, had offered to do it for her, being her first day on the job and all.

After waiting for exactly two minutes, as to not be overly suspicious, we approached him.

"Can we go to the toilet please, Mr Marston," asked Primrose, angelically.

"Both of you?" he grinned, displaying a smile so wide it was surprising his face did not split in two.

"Yes, I need a wee and Lainey needs…"

"I don't need to know what Lainey needs this time, thank you, Primrose," said Mr Marston. "Hurry up then."

Mr Marston was as easy to get around as a spinning roundabout.

Primrose and I entered the building, continuously looking around to see if anyone was watching. All clear apart from Miss Goggins, but she was busy on the phone and was paying no attention. She was no threat to us anyway.

Quickly, we darted into our classroom. We had hatched our plan over the weekend, and each knew our roles to a tee. Primrose rushed over and hopped straight onto the desk. I too then hopped onto the desk and placed my legs over Primrose's shoulders and shuffled around until I felt secure, like a piece of Lego sticking onto another. Now, with myself being the biggest of the pair, Primrose, by right, should really have been on my shoulders, but I needed to see up in that crawl space with my own eyes. Besides, Primrose was deceptively strong, and she could take my weight.

I was ready. Between my teeth I held the small torch that I had borrowed from my Dad's tool shed - I did not know how dark it would be up there – and Primrose's phone was secure in my right hand.

"Okay, Lainey, on the count of three," said Primrose.

"One, two."

On the count of two and a half, the door swung open and into the room marched Miss Black, the sound of her pointed heels rattling on the hard floor like a hammer driving into a nail.

"What on Earth are you doing?" she snapped.

Miss Black and I always had a great relationship. She was a beautiful teacher as well as a beautiful lady, and I knew she thought of me as her pet, but, for the first time ever, she sounded a little bit irked with me.

Primrose lowered me down from her shoulders and we climbed down from the desk.

"Miss, I know you said that it wasn't murder, but look," I said, pointing to the ceiling. "That tile is a little bit darker than the others. It has been flipped over. Someone was up there."

Miss Black looked at the ceiling tile and then she looked at me.

"I don't think it is any darker than the others," she said, her voice still sounding rather frosty.

"It is definitely darker," I said. "It's been turned over. I am one hundred percent sure about it."

Miss Black sighed one of her gentle sighs. "You aren't going to let this go, are you?" she asked.

I shook my head. "Never. I will not rest until I find the killer!"

Look, I do understand that some of the things surrounding Miss Mangle's death are a little unusual, but I'm sure there is some reasonable explanation for them all," said Miss Black. She paused, as if she were thinking very carefully about what she was about to say. "Look, I probably shouldn't be saying this, but I had my suspicions too, at first. Mr Wallace has been acting so strange of late and he was not in the staffroom when it all happened, but I talked myself around. I knew it was ridiculous to even be thinking such things about such a nice man. So, if I learned to let it go and move on, then you can too." Miss Black then came closer and placed her hand on my shoulder and gently said. "Please, Lainey, you must let this go and you must promise not to try and go up to the crawl space. It is far too dangerous for a child. It is an accident waiting to happen, and I couldn't bear it if anything happened to either of you. And I won't report you to Mr Wallace if you promise."

"Okay, Miss," I said. "But will you let us know if you see or hear anything suspicious about the case?"

Miss Black smiled and nodded. "I will, girls. Now, run along."

Primrose and I trudged over to the door, a heavy burden of disappointment and frustration weighing me down. I had barely left the classroom when it suddenly hit me. The W on the piece of paper – Miss

Mangle could not have been writing Wallace, could she?

Mr Wallace

It was the day of Miss Mangle's funeral. School was open but running with a skeleton staff. Most of the teachers were attending the ceremony and, while no children really wanted to go, the choir and an additional two pupils from every class had been volunteered to go to help bolster numbers, because with no family to speak of, and certainly no friends, there would probably be no-one else there.

Thankfully, I had escaped this torture. I could not have gone. I needed to stay. This was my chance to snoop around Mr Wallace's office and see if I could find anything. He would be gone for the entirety of the school day.

As always, I had hatched my plan well in advance and now I had to wait patiently for my opportunity, like a spider waiting for a fly to land in its web. I planted the seed in Miss Candy's mind right from the off. Whenever she glanced in my direction, I would give my tummy a little rub, being careful not to over-do it, as overacting a fake illness is the number one no-no. I had not said anything, just scattered the crumbs and hoped that Miss Candy would follow them. But now it was time to kick my plan into another gear. With fifteen minutes until break time, I sprang into action. I approached Miss Candy's desk as an assortment of children completed a vast number of worksheets left for them by their respective teachers.

"Excuse me, Miss," I said, in a normal voice, because putting on a fake sick voice is also another give away that you are not actually sick.

Miss Candy looked up.

"May I use the bathroom please?"

Miss Candy smiled and nodded. "Are you feeling alright today, Lainey," she asked quietly.

I had hooked my fish.

"Yes, I'm fine. I just have a bit of a tummy ache, but it's not too bad."

I departed the room and found myself in the corridor. I had a little time to play with, because with my tummy being 'sore', Miss Candy would not get suspicious if I took a longer-than-normal toilet break, but I had to act reasonably fast too, as I could not risk being caught.

I walked at a brisk pace down the corridor, treading softly to avoid my footsteps echoing around the school. I passed the girls toilets and took a sharp left. I could not hear anyone in the small school library, so I marched straight past and continued until I came to the door at the end of the corridor - Mr Wallace's office. I had been practicing how to pick a lock with a bobby pin by copying tutorials on Youtube. I had practiced for hours on end, opening the doors around my house using two pins, one as a pick and one as a lever, and while I was no expert, I had gained enough skill to open most doors in under three minutes. Doing it under stressful conditions, with slightly shaky and clammy hands may be a harder task though. I reached the door and retrieved the two picks from the left pocket of my trousers, but before I began, I instinctively pulled down the handle first to check if the door was even locked and, to my astonishment, it wasn't. The door breezed open inviting me in. If Mr Wallace was the murderer then he was either confident that he had already gotten away with it or had been very stupid in leaving his office unlocked.

Mr Wallace's desk was a mess. A big pile of papers spread over his desk like a tablecloth so you could barely see any of the wood underneath. A whole dishwasher load of coffee cups were scattered around the room. Some on the desk, some on the windowsill and a couple on the filing cabinet. It would not come as a huge surprise to find one underneath the rug on the floor! Some mugs were empty and enjoyed, some clearly started but forgotten about when things got hectic. Where to start?

I moved over to the desk and glanced over the paperwork. Invoices, bills, boring looking stuff from the Department of Education about this and that. Nothing really jumping out at me. Nothing screaming psychopath murderer on the rampage!

I opened the top drawer of his desk to see what treasures that held. Instantly, I recoiled. My heart skipped a beat. A book with an image of a giant tarantula, that looked a lot like Goliath, on the front cover. I picked it up. It was heavy. 'Rare and Deadly Spiders' was the title. I opened the book and it fell straight open to a page a little more than halfway through. The page must have been well read and the top left-hand corner of the page had been folded over a little, presumably to help the reader find it easily. And what was on that page took my breath away. A double page spread on the Black Widow spider!

And then it hit me like a freight train.

The W. Maybe it was not a name at all. Maybe Miss Mangle was writing widow. In black ink. BLACK WIDOW! My heart was racing. My head swimming. I needed to control myself. I needed to keep my mind clear. I focused on my breathing. In for four and out for four, in for four and out for four – just like we had learned in mindfulness class. It helped. My brain fog had cleared. This was my breakthrough!

Miss Mangle was found at her desk, right underneath her box of spiders. So perhaps Mr Wallace was up in the crawl space and, after putting some deadly poisonous black widow spiders into the box, he lowered it down onto her head, before raising it again when the deed was done? It was possible. While the box lowered with a touch of Miss Mangle's remote control, it could also be lowered manually by hand by simply pulling the rope down or up. So now Mr

Wallace had no alibi, and it seems that he had the means.

I closed the book and rummaged around the other drawers to see what else I could find. And there, in plain view, in the second drawer down, was a receipt from Archie's Rare and Exotic Arachnids in Perth, Australia. A bill for over three hundred pounds, paid for on the school credit card. This was getting weirder and weirder. The evidence growing ever more compelling. I turned my attention to the papers on the desk, moving them around to see if I had missed anything. And then, through the gaps in the papers, I saw something - two muddy footprints on the desk! I could not be sure that they belonged to Mr Wallace, but they looked the right size and it looked like the print from of a male shoe. Why would Mr Wallace be standing on the desk? The light bulb was on the other side of the room. I could see no other explanation other than he must have been stood on the desk to lift a ceiling tile and get up into the crawl space, before making his way over to our classroom and killing Miss Mangle with a box of deadly spiders! The dominos were sure falling fast now. I now needed to see if our classroom could be reached from Mr Wallace's office.

I picked up Mr Wallace's chair and heaved it onto the desk. Then I clambered up onto the desk and then onto the chair. Once standing on the chair, I stretched up to lift the ceiling tile and I pushed it ajar. As I did so, the chair wobbled a little and gave me a fright. Oh, how I wish Primrose were here. Not only to help steady the chair but to help share the mental burden. This was a lot for an eleven-year-old to take on by themselves. And Primrose would have loved all this. She would have gotten such a rush. She was absolutely devastated to be at the funeral rather than here with me executing the plan, but that was the way it had to be, and I needed to do this by myself.

I steadied myself, before hopping up, to catch the steel frame that held in the ceiling tiles with both hands. I hauled myself up and found myself in the dusty crawl space. Using the metal frame in the same way a train would use a track, I began to shimmy along in the direction of my classroom. I knew I was headed in roughly the right direction, but I was disorientated. There were no walls or corridors or markings up here, just a big open and stuffy space. The air was stale and dank. And it was dark. So, I trusted my other senses. I listened. I could hear the mumbled sound of Mr Marston's voice beneath me. He was reading his class a story about a boy and his pet T-rex and, from the roars of laughter; it sounded a jolly good read. My classroom was opposite his, just a little further back. I moved along. Eventually, Miss Candy's voice came into earshot and here is where I stopped. Using my fingernails, that seemed to have gotten a lot shorter over the past week or so, I caught faint hold of one of the ceiling tiles and lifted it ever so gently. I pressed my eye to the small opening I had made. There, beneath me, was my classroom! I replaced the ceiling tile and followed the light that shone up through the missing ceiling tile, back into Mr Wallace's office. I climbed down, maneuvered the tile back into place, put back the book and receipt and re-arranged the papers the best way I could. And then, after giving the room one final glace, I left. I had gone in unsure of what I would find. I had left discovering who had murdered Miss Mangle and how they had done it!

The Hospital or the Police Station?

"You don't look sick, and you're not hot," she said, pressing her hand against my head. "But we better get you to the doctors right away."

My imaginary sickness had taken a turn for the worse after discovering that Mr Wallace had committed murder! I needed to get out of school at once, so the rule about being subtle when faking your illness went out the window. I needed to ham it up. Mild stomach pangs quickly turned into crippling intestinal pains. Clutching my right-hand side and groaning in agony was more than enough to send a phone call home because of a suspected appendicitis. I was like a proper Shakespearean thespian the way I pulled it off.

I needed to get out of there pronto and share my discovery with P.C Herman as soon as possible. Normally Primrose would be the one I would share everything with first, but today I did not have time for all that. Murder is too serious a matter.

"I don't need the doctor, Mum," I said. "I'm not sick. I was just faking it. I think I know who killed Miss Mangle and I think I know how they did it and I must go tell P.C Herman at once about it and…

"Lainey Grayson, this is not like you at all," said my Mum, and I knew she was cross because she used my full name. "Faking an illness to get out of school? And what is this ridiculous talk of murder- you cannot be serious? Poor Miss Mangle is being buried today and as far as I am aware there is no investigation into her death. She just died of natural causes." Mum shook her head as she glared out of the windscreen. "I am not going to P.C Herman with all this nonsense."

"It's not nonsense," I said. "I have proof and I am going to go to P.C Herman whether you take me or if I have to go alone. There's been a murder and I need to solve it."

I could see Mum's vice like grip of the steering wheel relaxing a little. Her knuckles were a less deathly shade of white than they were a few seconds ago. She was wilting. Time for one more push. "Mum, I'm a good kid, aren't I? I always do my homework and I never get in trouble in school. My bedroom is usually in a reasonable condition and I am not spoiled, and I never bother you with much. So, just this once, can you please help me? Can we please go to the police station?"

Mum reached the crossroads. Home was right. She indicated left. She was going to the station! This was all happening so fast, like a snowball rolling the hill, getting bigger and bigger and bigger. And here I was, near the bottom of the mountain.

My Mum and I were silent as we got out of the car and walked up to the entrance of the police station. We remained quiet as we opened the doors and approached the front desk to the police officer on duty. The chap on duty sported a beard and moustache even bushier than P.C Herman's. It was as if he had coated his face in glue before rolling around on the floor of a busy barber's shop. It seemed that to be a police officer in our local area having wild facial hair was essential. It would not have been a huge surprise to see a female officer appear sporting a goatee.

"Is P.C Herman about?" asked my Mum before I had a chance to ask the very same question.

"And what is it regarding?" His words somewhat muffled through his facial forest.

"It's about, a possible murder," she said, sounding awfully embarrassed to be saying such a thing.

The officer just stared at my Mum for a moment, before standing and walking off through a door to his right. I knew from previous visitations that it led to P.C Herman's office. Moments later, the officer returned with P.C Herman in tow. He sighed when he saw me.

"In here, Lainey," he said, shooing me into his office.

My Mum and I entered the room. P.C Herman ambled around toward the back of his desk. Luckily, there were two chairs, so both my Mum and I took a seat. I could see my Mum's hands clamped firmly onto the arm rests, as if she were a nervy patient in a dentist chair.

"Lainey, we talked about this on the day it happened. Miss Mangle wasn't murdered." he said in his gravelly voice.

"But I found evidence," I said. "Solid evidence. It was in Mr Wallace's desk. He had a book about poisonous spiders. There was a page about black widows that had a corner folded over. It had been well examined. That must have been what Miss Mangle was writing when she died. You see, Miss Mangle had a box of spiders that hung from the ceiling and she used to lower the box and put our heads in there. I reckon Mr Wallace put in some poisonous spiders and lowered it until her head popped in, at which point she was bitten by a swarm of deadly arachnids and died. It makes sense as the ceiling tile above her desk is a slightly different colour to the others, which suggests that someone was up there, looking down, and when they replaced the ceiling tile, they put it back the wrong way, which is why the tile is not as faded from the sun as the other tiles. That must be why her thumb was pointing up. She was telling us that someone was up in the crawl space. And as well as having the means, Mr Wallace had opportunity. He was not in the staff room at break time. And he can access the crawl space from his office - I know because I checked. And he had more than enough time to pull it all off. And I saw muddy footprints on his desk, which proves he went up there. And, and, and... and I think that's it."

P.C Herman had seemingly turned into stone because he did not move or say anything for absolutely ages, but eventually he wrinkled his one huge uni-brow.

"Lainey, that sounds preposterous! What do you mean your teacher had a box of spiders that she put on your head? Do you know how crazy that sounds? Do you know anything about this," said P.C Herman, addressing my Mum.

My Mum was as white as an anaemic ghost. "First I've heard of it," she said, her voice all croaky. "But, and I don't like speaking ill of the dead, I do know that all the kids were scared stiff of her. I know Lainey has not been happy in her class. The other parents all say the same."

"Look, Lainey," said P.C Herman. "Even if I was to believe all this stuff about your teacher being this horrible child torturer and take all this evidence you have supposedly found on face value, then it doesn't really explain why we found no evidence ourselves. Surely if Miss Mangle were bitten by poisonous spiders then their bite marks would have been apparent on her face?"

"Maybe you missed them," I said. "It wouldn't be hard. I mean Miss Mangle's face was as wrinkled as an elephant's butt and her skin was covered in those horrible big brown liver spots that lots of old fogies get. Missing a small spider bite would not be beyond the realms of imagination, would it? Maybe you can go and check her body again and see if you can find anything upon closer examination."

P.C Herman looked at his watch and then at the clock on the wall to confirm. "It's her funeral today, isn't it?" he asked.

"Yes," I said, "and it has probably already started. But if you go now you may be able to examine her body before she is buried. Please, P.C Herman," I begged, "is there not a small part of you that thinks this is rather odd, a small part of you that wonders if there has been some sort of foul play? Well, if so, then this is our last chance to prove it. If you do not do anything, Mr Wallace is going to get away Scot free."

"Well, it is quiet here today." said P.C Herman.

He was in! "But listen very carefully to me, Lainey. If I do manage to examine her body and find nothing amiss, then this must be the absolute end of it. And you must not darken my doorstep again for a very, *very* long time!"

"That's fine, that's fine, "I said hurrying over to P.C Herman and helping him up from his chair. I grabbed his coat from the hanger behind him and helped him put it on before escorting him to the door.

"I'm off out, Greg," he said to his moustached mate on the front desk, "I'll be back in a couple of hours. I have my phone if you need me."

And then we all left. P.C Herman in his car and my Mum and I in ours.

Now it was a waiting game.

The Next Day

The waiting game had lasted longer than expected. I had spent the evening hoping that P.C Herman would arrive at my door after the funeral to update me on proceedings. But he never came. I had hardly slept with wondering if he had found anything, whether-or-not the case was closed or re-opened. And it was not just me who was a bundle of nerves - Primrose had been texting me all night long, fishing for updates, and I heard my Mum pacing the landing a few times in the night too.

I really did not want to be in school today. My head wasn't in it. I wanted to be back at the police station grilling P.C Herman about whether he had found any spider bites on Miss Mangle, but my Mum had said, "No way, not in a million years," which is about how long it felt since the whole case exploded into action.

When I did arrive in school that morning, things seemed strange from the off. You could feel it the minute that you set foot into the building. A strange atmosphere hung over the place like a dark blanket, covering everything in doubt and mystery. Teachers were darting in and out of rooms, whispered conversations held in the corridors. Deliberately blank expressions gave nothing away. It was all very cloak and dagger. While yesterday I had pretended that my stomach was dodgy, it really was in knots today, mostly because I had noticed that Mr Wallace's blue saloon was not in the car park when we arrived. It was the first thing I looked for coming in. Perhaps there was a reasonable explanation for it - a flat tyre, a burst water pipe at home and we were still catching the tail end of flu season. But what if it wasn't one of these things?

Most would not have approached Miss Sidebottom to ask such a question, but Primrose, as per usual, was as bold as brass.

"Where's Mr Wallace today, Miss?" she asked, without even a how do you do.

Miss Sidebottom began to cluck around like a hen about to lay a double-yolker.

"He's… he's… It's not my place to say and it doesn't concern you, so stop being so nosy and run along to class before I put you on detention," she barked.

When Mr Marston only gave us a half-smile as he wondered from the staffroom to his classroom, I knew something was dreadfully wrong. And I also knew that if anyone would be straight with me about what was happening it would be Miss Black.

Upon entering her classroom, we found her at her desk, sipping a cup of tea from a small fine china cup. The delicious smell of peppermint drifted through the air and the winter sun streamed through the large window onto her unblemished skin, giving her the appearance of a Victorian porcelain doll. Miss Black was sat peacefully, staring out of the window into the distance, no doubt thinking about something important and intellectual.

She was so deep in her own thoughts that I felt bad about interrupting her but interrupt her I did.

"What's going on, Miss?" I asked. "Where is Mr Wallace?"

Miss Black looked at us as if she were thinking very carefully about the next words that would leave her lips. "I shouldn't really tell you this, and if I do tell you, you must not repeat it to anyone else, as I'll get into big trouble, although everyone is going to find out soon enough anyway. Nothing like this could be kept secret for long."

"What is it, Miss?" I said, trying to hurry her along. I was fit to burst.

"Mr Wallace was arrested last night."

Our jaws hit the floor.

"Are you serious? What happened?" I asked, desperate for more information.

"We don't know all the details yet, but apparently the police had re-examined Miss Mangle's body just before she was buried and found some bite marks on her face and neck, which they had missed in their initial examination. They believe that they were caused by a cluster of poisonous spiders and for some reason they suspected Mr Wallace of having something to do with it all. And then later, when they went to his house to question him, they apparently found a shoebox full to the brim of black widow spiders in his garage, so they arrested him on the spot."

I was in shock. Complete shock. I felt like I had been hit by a freight train. "How do you know all this, Miss?" I managed to mutter.

"His wife rang in this morning and spoke to Miss Sidebottom. She briefed the rest of the staff. His wife cannot believe it, the teachers cannot believe it. I cannot believe it! He is one of the nicest people I have ever met. But then, apparently the police believe they have uncovered some wrongdoing and the evidence seems pretty compelling against Mr Wallace. I guess you just never know." And she once again looked out of the window, perhaps looking for the answers blowing in the wind.

The Letter

It was now official. Mr Wallace had been charged with the murder of Miss Mangle. Miss Sidebottom had only told us in morning assembly that Mr Wallace was not going to be in school for a while. She never said why but we all knew the reason. And it was not because Primrose and I had spilled the beans - the whole town was talking about it. Mr Wallace's arrest was plastered on the front of every local rag and reported on by every local news channel on T.V. There he was, P.C Herman, telling the whole world that a local man had been arrested and charged in connection with the murder of a teacher from Marden Vale School.

And while the whole thing was ghastly, my over-riding feeling was one of annoyance. It was I who had cracked the case. I was the one who worked out who had done it, and how it happened, and I was the one who had given this information to P.C Herman. But my involvement had not been mentioned once in print, I had not been featured in any news report and my name hadn't even passed the lips of any busy-body local discussing the case on the streets. I was furious about not getting the credit I deserved, and I had gone into the police station to say as much to P.C Herman but he was having none of it. He brushed me off, saying that he was not allowed to discuss anything about the case with a minor, especially now that a man had been charged with such a serious crime. The cheek! This was my case, not his.

I had been so caught up in feeling sorry for myself that I barely noticed the letters dropping onto the doormat about ten minutes before leaving for school on Friday. But when I did gather up the post, I noticed that one of the letters was addressed to me. I had no idea what the letter was about, and I was keen to see what was inside of it, but I waited until I had collected Primrose on the way to school before daring to open it. Primrose was still mad about missing all the drama and excitement on the day I had made my discovery. She had missed the rush of finding clues in Mr Wallace's office and the adrenaline hit of rushing to the police station to inform P.C Herman of my findings. Being the thrill seeker that she was, she was gutted about it, so I had promised to make sure that she did not miss anything else exciting linked to a case. And while I had no idea what was held within that bog-standard brown envelope, odds were that it had something to do with a case for our detective agency.

Eventually we came to the small red-brick wall surrounding Mrs Perkins's house at the corner of Washington Avenue, the street that led up to the school. The waiting wall is what locals called it. A nice low wall - bench height really - it proved an ideal meeting place for kids to swap soccer cards or play conkers or just hang around before and after school. Parents would congregate there too and have a natter before collecting their little darlings. Goodness knows what Mrs Perkin's thought of it all, but she never said anything, and she never got builders in to make the wall higher, so everyone took this as meaning she was fine with it.

Primrose and I made ourselves comfortable on the wall. We looked at each other, before I pushed my pinkie under the flap of the envelope and forced my finger upwards to rip it open and release the letter. We took hold of the piece of paper with one hand each and began to read.

Dear Lainey,

By now you will have heard of my arrest for the murder of Miss Mangle. I pray that you do not believe these ridiculous charges, because you, I fear, are my only hope.

Despite my claim of being innocent, the police seem happy that they have their man and even my lawyer thinks that I did it. She says there is so much compelling evidence against me that I should plead guilty now, which would lessen my jail time. But I refuse to go to jail for one single minute. Not for something I did not do!

The police believe that Miss Mangle was killed by being bitten by a cluster of black widow spiders. Apparently, they found a book about black widows in my office and a box of these spiders in my garage. Lainey, please believe me, I have never seen a black widow spider in my life. The book and the box of spiders must have been planted. I do not know who would do such a thing, but I swear to you that Miss Mangle's murder had absolutely nothing to do with me.

I know I was in my office the whole of break time, so I do not have an alibi, but that is because I got an e-mail earlier in the week saying that I was going to receive an important phone call from a school inspector at 11 a.m. on that day, so I waited in my office to receive the call, but no phone call came.

Lainey, I have a wife and three young children. I am a regular church goer I am a nice and a good person. Why would I do this? I am not a killer - I'm a vegan for heaven's sake!

Please Lainey, I know this is a lot to ask of a child, but my last hope rests with you. I know you have a brilliant mind and a fantastic detective agency, so if you could please just think about who could have done this and investigate the matter, not just for me, but also for my family and for the memory of poor Miss Mangle.

Lainey, I have been framed and there is a murderer walking free right now. They must be stopped!

Yours sincerely,

Mr Wallace

We lowered the note.

"What do you think?" said Primrose.

"I have to say, I think he has a point," I said. "It is something that has been niggling away at me for the past few days. At first, I got swept up in the excitement about catching Mr Wallace, but he is right. Why would he have left the book in his desk in an unlocked office? And why would he have not destroyed the spiders rather than leaving them to be found in his garage? Even if he had thought that he had got away with it, he surely would not have left all that evidence in plain sight. It is amateurish. And it is all too obvious. And another thing that has been bugging me is why did the police not spot the bite marks on Miss Mangle on the initial examination? It doesn't make sense."

"What are you saying?" asked Primrose.

"I'm saying that there is every possibility that Mr Wallace has been framed. I think we need to re-open the case!"

Who Next?

So, if Mr Wallace was not the murderer then it would mean going back to the drawing board (again) to find a new prime suspect. This time however the list of suspects was greatly reduced. With a sophisticated and clever method of murder established, a potentially phony e-mail from the school inspector to ensure that Mr Wallace was in his office at the time to give him no alibi, all signs pointed to an adult, rather than a child, committing the crime. Therefore, the best place to start would be to find out if anyone else, other than Mr Wallace, was absent from the staff room at break time on the day it happened.

Now, there were only two teachers in the school that I would feel happy in approaching to ask such a question and be confident that they would give us the truth. We couldn't ask Mr Marston though, as he was on duty in the yard, so it was once again down to Miss Black to be my sounding board.

"I see you more now than I did last year, girls," she said, as Primrose and I approached her desk before school began.

"Was there anyone other than Mr Wallace absent from the staffroom on the day Miss Mangle was murdered?" I blurted out. As usual I was a subtle as a jack hammer.

"And why do you need to know that?" asked Miss Black.

I placed my hands upon Miss Black's desk and leaned in, before whispering. "It's because I don't think it was Mr Wallace that murdered Miss Mangle. I think he's been framed."

Miss Black gently shook her head, her golden hair cascading around her slight shoulders. "He has not been framed, Lainey," she said, exasperated. "There is so much evidence against Mr Wallace that it is unbelievable that you are even considering someone else. It is one hundred percent - him!"

"Are you not even a little bit suspicious?" I asked, surprised that Miss Black did not see the evidence against Mr Wallace as all a bit too convenient herself.

"Not in the slightest. Now, girls, you did a brilliant job in helping catch Mr Wallace. But it is finished now. There is no more excitement to be had, no more games. It's over."

She looked at us and widened those sapphire blue eyes and nodded her head as if to put a huge full stop at the end of the sentence she had just uttered. Miss Black once again came across as if she wanted rid of us. She and I used to share the greatest bond, but throughout this case I kept getting the feeling that I was an annoying blue bottle buzzing around her head. Primrose and I turned and walked away. We would have to find out from another source if another teacher were not in the staffroom on the morning that Miss Mangle died. As we headed out of the classroom, we passed Miss Sidebottom, who strode like a sergeant major towards Miss Black's desk. A piece of paper was being strangled in her hand.

"Morning," she said abruptly, as she stomped towards Miss Black. And then, as she slammed the piece of paper down on her desk, she said, "I have a form here about the museum trip that requires your signature, if you wouldn't mind, Wendy."

Breathing Should be Easy

"Just breathe, Lainey."

It sounds so easy, but at this moment in time, something as simple as inhaling and exhaling seemed like rocket science. It felt like my chest was being sat on by an elephant. And a fat one at that! As I sat on the lavatory in the girl's toilet with Primrose rubbing my back, a thousand thoughts swam around in my head like a huge school of fish, all clamouring for attention. Pieces of the puzzle that I had somehow missed, until now, popped in and out of my consciousness.

Primrose had been calm and helpful up 'til now, but she was now growing hungry for answers as to why I was so panicked and flustered.

"Lainey, what's the matter?"

What was the matter? Everything – that's what!

By now I had managed to catch my breath and compose myself just enough to begin to form sentences.

"What if it wasn't widow or Wallace that Miss Mangle was writing? What if it was Wendy? Wendy, in black! Wendy Black!"

The minute that Miss Sidebottom had uttered her name the whole thing had come crashing down upon me like a ton of bricks.

"Miss Black?" said Primrose, clearly shocked to hear me say her name as I had never once said anything negative about Miss Black ever before. Quite the contrary. But now I seemed to be accusing her of the most fiendish of all crimes.

"Think about it - Miss Black was the one who found us in the classroom, so she must have been in and around the corridor at the time. She certainly was not in the staffroom. And the fact that she ran over to Miss Mangle."

Primrose stared at me with big green eyes.

"She never runs. Miss Black always wears high heels. But she could not have been wearing them that day - she must have been wearing trainers. Maybe to help her move around school quickly? And she felt Miss Mangle's neck for a pulse. She stroked her forehead."

"And what's strange about that?" asked Primrose. "She was just checking to see if Miss Mangle was dead, wasn't she?"

"Perhaps. Or perhaps she was rubbing something onto the spider bites to conceal them. Make up or something similar. Do you not think it was strange that no one noticed the bites the first time round but when P.C Herman examined her body on the day of the funeral they were there?"

Primrose looked bemused. "But why would she want to hide the spider bites if she was just going to frame Mr Wallace anyway?"

"Maybe she wasn't planning to frame Mr Wallace," I said. "Maybe she thought she would get away with it. Framing him may have only arisen as a plan once you and I began sniffing around. It makes sense. Once we were on the case Miss Black would have known we would have not given up until someone was caught."

Now it was Primrose's turn to draw a huge intake of breath. "This is huge," she said.

"Huge," I said back.

"Primrose," I said, still not quite having gathered my thoughts properly, "have I been really stupid? Have we been hoodwinked? Did we send an innocent man away? "

"Well, that's what we are going to find out, isn't it?" Primrose replied.

Miss Black

It wouldn't be her. It couldn't be her. As hard as it was to believe that Mr Wallace had killed Miss Mangle, Miss Black having done it was even more implausible. And to believe she could then frame Mr Wallace for it was like a poisoned cherry on top of the cake. But at the same time, there were loose ends in the case that needed to be tied up. Why Miss Black was in the corridor the day it all happened and why she was not wearing high heels, being the main ones.

"Why don't we just ask her straight out?" Primrose suggested. "She may have some reasonable explanation for it all and we can finally put this case to bed."

"We can't do that," I said. "If it were her, she would have probably thought up a fantastic lie to cover her tracks by now. She is a genius after all."

"So, what will we do? Will we ask another teacher to confirm that she wasn't in the staffroom on the day it happened?" Primrose asked.

"We could do," I said. "But who would we ask?"

And then we were interrupted by a loud pounding on the door.

"What are you doing in there?" came the frantic voice from outside. "Hurry up, will you. I'm bursting here."

It was time to leave. It was probably for the best that we were disturbed – the girl's toilet was not the most glamorous, or the most secure of places to be discussing the delicate matters of this case.

I got up, threw back the latch to the toilet and opened the door. As Primrose and I shuffled out, Ava Cunningham rushed past us, almost knocking us to the floor. She slammed the door behind her and let out a satisfying cooing sound, as if she had just ran a marathon across the hot desert sand in bare feet and had just plunged them into a bowl of iced water.

As we left the bathroom and re-emerged into the corridor, another thought crossed my mind. Instead of asking a teacher about it, we could have another stab at gleaning some information from Mrs Goggins. It was a long shot, an awfully long shot, but maybe we would get lucky. After all, people do win the lottery, get struck by lightning twice and defy other incredible odds. And I would much prefer to approach the lovely Miss Goggins with all this rather than one of the other teachers. Besides, while one of the teachers may be able to say how long Miss Black was out of the staffroom for, they probably would not be able to say what she was doing during that time. Mrs Goggins on the other hand would surely have seen her if she were slipping in and out of rooms and doing anything untoward. It was just a case of whether she could remember.

I glanced down at my watch. 9:17. Three minutes until lessons began. Not long, but it was better than waiting until break time. I could not bear to hang on that long. Besides, most of the pupils and staff were in their classrooms by now and the corridor was nice and quiet, so hopefully we could interrogate Mrs Goggins without interruption.

As we approached Mrs Goggin's office area, we could see that she still had her coat on. A big, thick, woolly thing it was, and it made her look rather like a giant Koala (notice I did not say bear- as Koala's are actually not bears, they are marsupials).

"Morning, Mrs Goggins," I said, as brightly as I could manage.

"Morning, girls. And how are we today?"

"We're spiffing," I said. Mrs Goggins always used old words like these so I knew she would like it. Soften her up for upcoming grilling.

"Mrs Goggins," I said coyly, "I know we asked you about the day that Miss Mangle died already, but could we ask you a couple more questions? It really is so important."

"I'll try my best, dear, but I can't promise anything," said Mrs Goggins, looking rather similar as a concussed goldfish.

I took a deep breath before asking. "Do you remember Miss Black being on the corridor on the day Miss Mangle died? And do you remember anything unusual about Miss Black in general – the way she was acting, what she was wearing. Anything at all! Please, can you try and remember. It really is a matter of life and death."

And that was true. It was Mr Wallace's life and Miss Mangle's death.

"Oh, that sounds very serious," said Mrs Goggins. "Right then, I'll have a little think."

And then it was as if the lights had gone out in Mrs Goggin's head. Her body was still there but her mind had seemingly gone on a two-week vacation to Venice. She just sat there with a blank expression, staring far into the distance as if searching for something far, far away. But then she began to slowly scrunch up her forehead until her face took on an extraordinary prune like quality. Suddenly, her face exploded back into life.

"Oh yes, I do remember seeing Miss Black that day, the poor thing."

"What do mean the poor thing?" Primrose asked.

"Well, she rushed into the staff toilet first thing at break time and stayed in there an awfully long time. Right up until the time she came out and discovered poor Miss Mangle. I think she had a little..." and she gentled patted her stomach twice.

"Had a little what?" said Primrose, a little more firmly this time.

"You know, a dickey tum-tum," she whispered, so low that it was barely audible.

"A what?" Primrose asked.

Mrs Goggins sighed and shook her head as if pained to spell it out in black and white.

"She had the trots, girls. The skitters, the squits, the runs. She was making stinky bum gravy. She had terrible diarrhoea!"

Well, there was no confusion about what Mrs Goggins meant now!

"How do you know?" I asked.

Mrs Goggins then started nibbling at her bottom lip, like a squirrel gnawing on an acorn. "I don't know if I should be telling you this. I'm not sure I should be saying anything delicate about a teacher to you girls."

"Please, Mrs Goggins," I pled. "I wouldn't ask if it weren't so important. And you know me, I love Miss Black, I wouldn't say anything to embarrass her."

This seemed to satisfy Mrs Goggins. She released her bottom lip from between her teeth and moved in really close to the open window of her office, "Well, between you and me, she was making a terrible racket. I could hear the whole thing from way out here. It sounded like a brass band was rehearsing in there, what with all the squeaks and booms and what not. She must have had a terrible dose of it."

"Thank you, Mrs Goggins," I said. "Most…informative."

"Not at all girls," Mrs Goggins said warmly. "I'm glad I could be of help."

I looked at my watch. Bang on 9:20. If we did not get to class right away, we would be in trouble, not that that worried me anymore. It is not as if my head was going to be forced into a spider tank for being a few minutes over. So, instead of rushing to class, Primrose and I made a little trip to the female staff toilet. Slowly, I opened the door and we both poked our heads inside. Yes, as I suspected, there were ceiling tiles here too, and if someone were to stand on the cistern at the back of the toilet, they could easily clamber up into the crawl space, providing they were young, slim and reasonably in shape, which Miss Black certainly was.

"So, what do you think, Lainey?" asked Primrose.

"She could have had a bad tummy. It happens," I said. "And Mrs Goggins heard her in there, so it's not like Miss Black was completely unaccounted for."

Primrose shook her head. "It's too much of a coincidence. It is like she was setting herself up with an alibi. She could have easily downloaded some pooping noises, like the recording I have of the police siren, and then connected her phone to a small portable speaker. That wouldn't be hard to do."

"I suppose you're right," I said. "Well, we don't know if she really did have a bad tummy on the day, but we do know that she had the time and the opportunity to do it. But we cannot prove anything, yet. We need something else. Something more concrete!"

Finding More Evidence

Back in the olden days, digging the dirt on someone would involve following them secretly, covertly watching their every move in the aim of uncovering clues. Acquaintances would be interviewed on the sly and slowly and surely the detective would gather a body of evidence against a suspect. But now you could find out a wealth of information just by surfing the internet. If a person has any sort of social media account, you could potentially find out a lot about them from snooping through their profiles. Unfortunately, while Miss Black was on a few sites, she was not particularly active and had set the strongest possible security settings, so we could not glean as much information as we would have liked. Primrose and I tried a different approach - we simply typed her name, Wendy Black, into Google. Instantly a gallery of faces belonging to a whole host of ladies named Wendy Black popped up. But none of them were our Wendy Black. We then scrolled down to the list of websites beneath the photos to see if we could find any information. Again, we drew a blank. There was an interior designer named Wendy Black and another Wendy Black who was curator of archaeology at a South African museum, but nothing about any teacher named Wendy Black. So, we began to type in a few other bits of information that we knew about her - the street she lived on and where she went to university – Nothing! But when we hit the enter button after typing in her previous school, St Edmund's, something of interest did catch our eye. It was a report from the Gazette and Herald, a paper servicing the neighbouring county of Wiltshire. Primrose clicked into the article and we began reading it with great interest.

Tributes have been pouring in over the sudden death of primary school teacher, Mrs Shapiro, who sadly passed away at St Edmund's School early yesterday morning.

It is understood that Mrs Shapiro was eating a bowl of cornflakes in the staffroom before school when she started choking. Despite best efforts from the staff members that were present, they were unable to revive her and she passed away.

P.C Munster said, "Mrs Shapiro had a severe allergy to nuts and initial reports suggest that she may have had some sort of reaction, but further tests will be conducted in due course."

The school Principal has said, "Our thoughts and sympathies are with Mrs Shapiro's family at this sad time. She was a wonderful person and an excellent teacher, and she will be greatly missed."

St Edmund's has remained closed for the past two days but is reopening this morning. Psychologists from the National Education Centre are advising teachers on how to help the pupils deal with the tragic event.

Mrs Shapiro's funeral is scheduled for Monday 15th May, at 2.pm at Holy Trinity Church. May she rest in peace.

"That's weird, "said Primrose. "A teacher dead in her last school and a teacher dead in her current school. And who knows where she was before St Edmund's, perhaps there is another dead teacher in that school, too."

"Let's stick to the facts we have," I said, even though my thoughts were also beginning to race away from me. "Admittedly, it is a bit unusual for two different teachers to die at two different schools that Miss Black has taught at, but it could also very well be a coincidence."

Primrose was having none of it.

"It's way too strange to be a coincidence. And look at the date - she left St Edmund's and came to us only months after all this happened. And what was the article saying about the teacher dying from an allergic reaction? Why would someone have an allergic reaction to nuts from eating cornflakes? There aren't any nuts in cornflakes, so how would one get there?" Primrose lifted a finger into the air. "I know, maybe she ate a Crispy Nut Cornflake. If it did then it could only have happened two ways; either a Crispy Nut Cornflake got into the regular cornflake packet in the factory where they are made, or the other option, which is more likely, is that it was put in there by someone on purpose. If someone wanted Mrs Shapiro dead, then that would be an easy way to bump her off."

"What are you suggesting?" I said, knowing full well what Primrose was suggesting.

"I am saying that I think Miss Black killed Miss Mangle and framed Mr Wallace and I think she killed this other teacher too by poisoning her cornflakes. I think we are dealing with a serial killer."

What Next?

Over the next few hours, Primrose and I had searched the internet to find out more details on Mrs Shapiro's death. The coroner's report had indeed confirmed that Mrs Shapiro had died of anaphylaxis, most likely as a result of eating a nut, but how this came about remained a mystery. The police had not charged anyone with any crime, and it was simply put down to a tragic accident. This was something that did not sit right with us. We hated loose ends.

With our internet information gathering finished, we had determined that our next step must be to contact St Edmund's school directly to try and see if we could get any information on the incident, and most importantly, if Miss Black were related to it in any way. We had to ring up St Edmund's during school time if we wanted to talk to the principal, so we had waited patiently until our break time, at which point we had taken position behind the lavender bush in the sensory garden. I rang the school on Primrose's phone and luckily the principal, Mrs Lovejoy, was available to chat. I pretended to be a principal from another school, and I asked Mrs Lovejoy about Miss Black's credentials, because I was considering her for a job. Mrs Lovejoy had only said good things - that Miss Black was a lovely lady and a terrific teacher, who displayed a great rapport with the children. However, I was not getting far in gleaning whether-or-not Miss Black had done anything suspicious regarding the death of Miss Shapiro and, with break time nearly over, I decided that I had to force the issue. It was hard to bring up the death of Miss Shapiro casually in conversation, but I mentioned that I had heard about was terrible event and said that Miss Black must have been upset by the whole thing. Mrs Lovejoy confirmed that this was the case. Then I asked if Miss Black was close to Mrs Shapiro. Mrs Lovejoy's response was that they were colleagues. When I asked if Miss Black was present when Mrs Shapiro died, Mrs Lovejoy's friendly manner quickly shifted into a suspicious short tone and the conversation was brought to a swift conclusion.

It was a shame. We would have liked another piece of evidence to add to the growing pile, but we still felt we had a compelling enough case against Miss Black to bring to PC Herman.

So that is exactly what we did. And here I found myself at the front desk of the police station, once again asking a half man-half werewolf creature, if I could speak with PC Herman. The minute that PC Herman stepped out of his office and saw Primrose and I standing there, he was clearly most displeased. Every muscle of his weathered face crinkled up tightly as if the very sight of us caused a bitter taste in his mouth. And his attitude was as sour as his face - he barely glanced in our direction and he did not greet us or welcome us in, He just walked back into his office and left the door open behind him. I think as an invitation to enter, albeit a cold one!

Primrose and I sat on one side of the desk, PC Herman on the other. P.C Herman leaned back on his chair and asked, "So what can I do for you today, Lainey?"

"We have some information that we think you will be very interested in regarding the Miss Mangle murder case," said Primrose quickly, sounding a little annoyed that P.C Herman had addressed me and not us as a pair.

PC Herman's face scrunched up even more after hearing this. He looked extraordinarily like a kiwi that had been sat in a fruit bowl for far too long. He then began huffing and puffing and shuffling around in agitation on his chair.

"I thought we had an understanding, Lainey!" he snapped at me, even though it was Primrose who had said it. "We agreed that we would not talk about this case again. I arrested Mr Wallace after the evidence you provided me with, and he is going to trial in a few weeks. There is a mountain of evidence against him already, so we do not need any more. In fact, you continuing to stick your nose into it may be harmful to our case at this point, so whatever you have to say- I don't want to hear it."

"But that's the whole point," said Primrose stubbornly, who did not seem the least bit intimidated by PC Herman's angry demeanour and aggressive tone, "we don't want Mr Wallace to get convicted for it, because it wasn't him that did it. It was Miss Black!"

And while PC Herman spent most of his life angry, I had never seen him like this before. His teeth were gritted together so hard that it was a wonder they didn't all shatter then and there. There was a fire in his eyes. He was like a teased bull, and we were dressed from head to toe in red.

"I...don't...want...to...hear...about...it...Lainey! "he said, his voice sounding like stones rattling in a jam jar.

Primrose however, blustered on. "Well, it was Miss Black that did it - we are sure of that. We discovered that she was not in the staff room at break time on the day it happened, she spent most of it locked in the staff toilet, and from there you can easily reach the crawl space in the ceiling, so she could have easily committed the crime. And when coupled with the fact that she wore trainers on the day rather than her usual high heels, the black W that we now think refers to Wendy Black, and that she was one the one who first entered the classroom and she rubbed Miss Mangle's face and neck, probably to conceal the spider bites with make-up or something similar, means that she, not Mr Wallace, must surely be the prime suspect. And that is not even mentioning the convenient amount of hard evidence against Mr Wallace that was placed in broad daylight, which surely pointed to him being framed and the fact…"

Primrose paused before hammering the final nail into Miss Black's coffin.

"…The fact that another teacher also died in Miss Black's previous school, also in mysterious circumstances means that Miss Black is not just the murderer of Miss Mangle, she is a serial killer!"

PC Herman rose from his chair and pounded over to the door. "Nonsense, girls!" he boomed, his face red as lava. "Mr Wallace is going to trial in a few days and a jury of adults will decide on his guilt, not two medalling girls. Now, I will not be undermined like this anymore. I do not want to hear any more about it, Lainey!" he bellowed, even though I had not uttered a single word since I stepped inside his office. "If you darken my doorstep again, I will be forced to arrest you for obstructing the course of justice. Now, good day!"

And the door was slammed firmly behind us.

We left the police station crestfallen. We had been sure that PC Herman would share our suspicions or at least consider the possibility.

What were we to do now? We could not give up at this stage, but with PC Herman not entertaining the evidence we had against Miss Black, we needed a new avenue. We needed something stronger to go back to

PC Herman with, something that would confirm her guilt beyond any reasonable doubt.

I knew that the vital piece of evidence would be proof that she sent the phony e-mail to Mr Wallace pretending to be the inspector, or if her internet search history showed that she had researched black widows or if she had visited Archie's Rare and Exotic Arachnids where the spiders had been purchased from, we would have her. But a clever and cunning woman like Miss Black would have surely deleted all her search history and getting hold of her laptop and figuring out her log on details would be like breaking into Fort Knox!

It felt as if she had us beaten. There really was only one thing left we could do.

We would have to try and nab her phone and she if we could find a file of pooping noises on it. That would give us proof that she may not have had a bad tummy on the day it happened and that she was just giving herself an alibi while she did the deed. Finding that file was our final hope. It was not going to be an easy mission, but we would give it our all!

The Best Plan We Had

I didn't have that Friday feeing today. Instead, I felt the anxiety of a Monday Morning in Miss Mangle's class, magnified by about one million. We had gotten in a few scrapes on our cases before, but attempting to steal a phone from a teacher, a teacher who could very well be a serial killer, was easily the scariest and most nerve-racking thing we had ever done in our detective careers to date.

Our plan was to get Miss Black out of her classroom with a ruse about there being something urgent that needs her attention. After leaving the room, we would nab her bag before rushing down to the police station with it in the hope that there would be a pooping sound effect, or something else incriminating, on her phone, that would give PC Herman another push into reopening the case and examining Miss Black more closely.

But it was not a fool proof plan by any means. Miss Black was not daft and there could very well be no digital fingerprints of her guilt on the phone. And if so, then she would most likely have got away with it. Plus, we would be in huge trouble. We would be most likely be suspended from school - possibly expelled! And that is without even considering if PC Herman was serious about arresting us if we poked our nose into the case again. But what was the alternative? Watching Mr Wallace get convicted and have him rotting away in jail for the rest of his life for something he probably did not do would be mental torture, as would knowing that I had not properly put to bed the biggest case of my life. This was something we simply had to do. It was our last hurrah!

We were in school ridiculously early, a good five minutes before the first keeners would normally enter the premises, but we wanted to be in before the mayhem of school started. The less people that were around the less likely we would be disturbed when executing our plan and the less likely we would be to get caught. Normally if Miss Black would have seen us in school this early it would have aroused suspicion, but we hoped that by telling her some gob smacking news it would distract her enough to ignore our early arrival and leave the room without her handbag and its precious contents.

We already knew that Miss Black was in school, as her car was in the car park, but was she in her classroom ready for us to execute our plan?

Primrose and I scanned the corridor. All clear. Then Primrose crouched down and scuttled underneath the window of the door to Miss Black's classroom. And then, as quick as a flash, Primrose popped her head up and glanced through the window before immediately shooting back down again.

"She's in there," she whispered, a tingle of excitement crackling in her voice. "She's at her desk, drinking her peppermint tea."

Primrose raised a finger, then two and then three, at which point we burst in.

"Miss Black, you must go to Miss Sidebottom's office, quick!" yelled Primrose, as if her life depended on it. "PC Herman is on the phone and he says that he needs to talk to you about Miss Mangle's murder. He says it's of the upmost importance."

And for the first time ever I saw Miss Black flustered. She placed down her tea in such a haphazard fashion that a little dribble spilled over the edge and pooled on her desk. She immediately shot up from her chair and trotted off at a brisk pace towards the door, rubbing her hands together all the way, as if worry were like mud on her hands that she could wipe off. She did not say anything to us, or even look at us as she passed, she seemed to too preoccupied with this mysterious (and imaginary) phone call from PC Herman. She was probably thinking that PC Herman has worked it all out and that she was in big trouble and was trying to think up excuses already. Miss Black left the room, and we could hear her clip clopping off toward Mr Wallace's office.

I had calculated that we only had about a minute until Miss Black would return after realising that no one was on the other end of the phone and that she had been scammed, so we had to move like lightening.

Primrose and I rushed over to her desk and grabbed her bag that hung on the back of chair. Primrose pulled open the bag and we could see that Miss Black's phone was in there, along with a lip stick, perfume, mascara, some foundation make-up and half a packet of extra-strong mints. Primrose reached in and grabbed the phone and stuffed it into her pocket. As we prepared to make a hasty retreat, we heard a noise coming down the corridor.

Clip-Clop!

It seemed I had slightly miscalculated by a few seconds.

"What were you doing rooting in my bag, girls?" said Miss Black, standing in the doorway.

Confrontation

We stood like little lambs before the big bad wolf. What were we to do now? Like before, I knew that Miss Black would not believe any falsehood from Primrose or I, so there was nothing else to do now but be honest.

"We know, Miss Black. We know you did it!" I said.

"Did what?" she said, even though I knew that she knew exactly what I meant.

"Kill Miss Mangle," said Primrose, "and then frame Mr Wallace for it. And we think you killed Mrs Shapiro from your last school, too."

Miss Black looked at us, but particularly at me. I knew what she was thinking. She knew that I, like her, would not be fooled by any tall tale when the truth was staring me straight in the face.

"You're right, girls," she said. "You are one hundred percent right."

My jaw dropped wide open. This could not be happening. My emotions swirled around me like frothy milk in a mug of hot cocoa. Here I was stood in front of my mentor, my hero, not knowing if she was about to now do me in!

"I knew it was only a matter of time until you found me out, Lainey. I have been anxious about it since the moment you said that you thought Miss Mangle was murdered. It is a relief that the truth is out there now. I knew the minute that you began sniffing around that you would eventually work it all out. Well done, you. You are truly brilliant."

I know Miss Black was a cold-blooded killer but being flattered by her still felt good.

"But why?" I asked. "I know Miss Mangle was horrible, but why kill her? And why did you kill Mrs Shapiro."

Miss Black smiled and stared deeply into my eyes. "You must understand this, Lainey. When you are so smart, as we are, life can be awfully boring. Talking to most people is pointless - they just cannot keep up. Everything that comes out of their mouth is so dreary and dull. Everyday life can be so tedious and mundane, so I need something to keep my mind sharp. And that is why I do it. I like to kill people in very clever and sophisticated ways and get away with it. It gives me a tremendous buzz to know I have outsmarted the detectives. I have done it a good number of times now. You have to admit, Lainey, this one was deliciously clever, wasn't it?" And when she smiled a star like twinkle shone from her eye. "But," and Miss Black held up her finger as if making a very serious point, "and I mean this, I only kill horrible people. And I mean *horrible* people. People who hurt animals, people who cheat old age pensioners out of money. People, like Miss Black, who are cruel to children. And I suppose by getting rid of bad people that means I could be considered a good person really. A modern-day Robin Hood."

"And what about Mr Wallace," snapped Primrose. "He's not a bad person. In fact, he is lovely, and he's in jail now for something you did."

Miss Black nodded her head.

"That part was unfortunate. I panicked. You see I knew Lainey was getting close to finding an answer and would not stop until she did, so I framed him for the crime. It was not personal. I always have a patsy lined up in case the police ever think there was a wrongdoing. But I have never had to use one, until now. I obviously never expected Miss Mangle to write the W before she died - the horrid old bat spotted me up in the roof, just before the spider box came down right on top of her." said Miss Black, rubbing her hands as if the mere thought of it made her feel warm and fuzzy inside. "Serves her right, after putting that spider box on the heads of you poor children. Luckily, she only got to write the W from my name before the spider poison killed her, it was a happy coincidence that it proved to be a fantastic piece of evidence that could be used against Mr Wallace."

Miss Black then paused and looked at us. She could tell that we were horrified.

"But, while I always have someone lined up to frame, should I need to, I would never let someone innocent go down for something that I did. Not if they didn't deserve it."

"Well, someone innocent has gone down for the crime, so what are you going to do about?" said Primrose, with her arms folded, as if she was a parent talking to a child rather than a child talking to a killer. "I assume you are going to turn yourself in now?"

"Not exactly," said Miss Black, "I actually have other plans in place."

"Other plans?" snorted Primrose, "Do tell."

"I am leaving tonight. I am heading to the airport straight after school and boarding a flight to Costa Rica to begin a new life. But before boarding the plane I was going to post a letter to PC Herman and confess my guilt. The police will set Mr Wallace free and then I would have the excitement of watching the police try to capture me, while I obviously outsmart them with a new identity. So, if you girls can ignore this conversation and just give me twenty-four hours then this whole thing will be done and dusted, once and for all. We can all get on with our lives, no harm done."

"No harm done!" said Primrose. "You must be joking. You are a beast. A monster!"

"No, she's not," I said, after standing silently, taking it all in, thus far.

"What?" scoffed Primrose "What are you on about, Lainey?" her face all twisted up in confusion.

"She's right." I said calmly. "Miss Mangle was horrible. She was absolutely horrible. She made all our lives miserable, every day. And she did the same with the class before us and the class before that and she would have done it to all the classes after us. No one misses her. In fact, the world is a better place now she is gone. I am sorry but that is the truth. Miss Black has done us all a favour. And, if Miss Black says that all the others were as ghastly as Miss Mangle, then I believe her. So, the way I see it if she confesses, then I am fine with it."

Primrose looked at me in a way she had never looked at me before. "I can't believe I'm hearing this," she said. "Lainey – she's a murderer."

"Things in life aren't always black and white, Primrose," I said. "And this is a classic case of that. Miss Black is a good person. I know she is. She was always so kind to us, wasn't she?"

"Well...yes, but that's not the point."

"I think it is," I said.

And then I gave Primrose the big eyes and all the time I kept saying in my head, play the police siren, play the police siren. I tried to send the message out of brain and through my eyes to Primrose and hoped beyond hope that she would receive it. You see, Primrose and I had this telepathy thing going on. It is like we always knew each other's thoughts or what the other one was feeling, even if we were miles away. It is the kind of bond that identical twins often have. And despite not being actual biological twins, we were such super-tight best friends, what we seemed to have the same intuition.

"But I'm so sorry, Miss Black, there's a problem," I said.

"What problem," asked Miss Black anxiously.

"I wish I had come to you first and had you explain it like you just did there. I just thought you were a ruthless murderer, so I told P.C Herman about our suspicions just before we arrived at school."

"It's okay. I understand, Lainey" said Miss Black with the soft look of new-born puppy rather than a mass murderer. "That does put a spanner in the works because if the police are looking for me, then I will not be able to board that flight, but don't worry, I'll find another way. It may take an extra day or two to reach Costa Rica though, so I will not be able to post the letter today, but it should not be too much longer for Mr Wallace to wait. Miss Black then reached out and gently took the bag from over Primrose's shoulder. "Right, this is it then, girls. It was a pleasure teaching you both. You are brilliant girls and I wish you every success in the future and I'll send you a postcard from Costa Rica!"

By now, Primrose had received my mental message.

"What's that noise?" said Miss Black.

"Oh no," it's too late, they're here already," I said, as the muffled sound of a police siren filled the air.

At once, Miss Black kicked off her shoes and dashed for the door.

"No, Miss," I said. "They are probably just around the corner. They will catch you for sure if you run. I have a better idea - get into the cupboard and I will lock the door. I'll tell the police that you've already made your escape, that you went on foot in the direction of the train station, and then, once they have gone to look for you, I'll let you out and you can drive to safety."

Miss Black looked at me for a moment and then at Primrose for a lot longer. "Primrose will tell them where I am."

"I won't!" said Primrose, "I don't like what you have done but I understand it. And if Lainey thinks that this is the right thing to do then I'll play along."

"I'm sorry, Miss Black, but you have to hurry. There really is no other choice. Getting in the cupboard is your only hope!"

While Miss Black was always so cool, calm and collected, she was clearly rattled now. I knew I had to act fast. Her judgement was temporarily impaired, and it was time to pounce. If we waited any longer, she would work out the police siren was coming from Primrose's pocket rather than from the road outside.

"Come on, get in," I said opening the door and pulling out some art supplies and document files to make a bit more space, "They'll be here any second."

Miss Black moved toward the open cupboard. I placed my hand on her back and guided her in gently.

"I'm sorry about this, Miss. But I'll get rid of them as soon as I can and then I'll let you out."

Miss Black squeezed herself into the cupboard and scrunched herself up into a ball. She looked up at me with wide hopeful eyes, like I was an adult, and she was a small child. I looked at her briefly, before shutting the door. My wrist snapped the key to the right, locking her in.

And then Primrose and I just hugged.

Arrested

It had been a strange start to the day to say the least! But it only got weirder as the day progressed. When other children began to filter into school and found that we had locked Miss Black into the cupboard, there was a mixed reaction. Most of the boys thought it was brilliant. One lad, Tom Tiddle, nearly wet his pants he was laughing so hard. However, some of the more sensible pupils had taken a dimmer view of it and alerted Miss Sidebottom. She was furious of course. I've never in my life seen someone's face turn as purple with anger as hers did when she came into the room and found myself and Primrose standing in front of the cupboard, while the muffled pleas from Miss Black, who was begging to be set free, came from inside. She was like an over ripe damson. She could barely speak with rage, but she managed to snarl the demand that we set Miss Black free at once!

Primrose refused and then she put the key to the cupboard into her mouth, after saying that she would swallow it whole if anyone approached her to try and get it.

I then explained the whole sorry story to Miss Sidebottom, while Miss Black professed her innocence from inside the cupboard. Of course, at this point,

Miss Sidebottom had no choice other than to ring the police.

PC Herman's face was even more purple than Mrs Sidebottom's when he arrived and saw what Primrose and I had done, but once we had explained to him that Miss Black had confessed to killing Miss Mangle, and with all the circus-show that was going on around him, he had no choice but to arrest Miss Black and at least question her.

Despite denying the whole thing once she was at the station, PC Herman at least took the time to delve into her past, and when he did, he found a string of deaths surrounded her, like horrid pearls on a deadly necklace. And then his suspicions were well and truly aroused. After getting the tech experts to trawl through Miss Black's laptop and phone, they found that Miss Black had set up a fake e-mail account and she had used it to masquerade as a school inspector and had messaged Mr Wallace, telling him to expect a call in his office at the time it all happened, thus setting him up with no alibi. They also found, in Miss Black's deleted items, a file of pooping noises that was downloaded from www.1001soundeffects.com, which proved beyond reasonable doubt that she did not have diarrhoea at all on the day it happened, and she was just giving herself an alibi. And after all these findings, the next step was to exhume Miss Mangle's corpse for further inspection. Upon detailed examination, the forensic scientists found minute traces of make up around the sites of the spider bites. It was the same brand of the foundation make up that Miss Black wore and was found in her handbag. It was concluded that she had used her make up to cover up the spider bites on the day she was murdered. She was bang to rights!

Mr Wallace had been released and it was she instead who was now sat in jail awaiting trial for not one, but seven, counts of murder, and the investigation continues.

Meanwhile everything else is getting back too normal. Well, normal-ish. There is still a weird vibe around town, and especially in school, what with the death of a teacher and the arrest of another one for her murder. But things were slowly and steadily returning to the way they were.

But life for Primrose and I had changed completely! It was gradual, at first. We had an article written about us in the local paper and had then been interviewed by a local news channel about how we cracked the case. And then the whole thing exploded! The national press got hold of the story and we were on the front of every newspaper across the land. The public went mad for it. They lapped up the story like a cat licking cream from a saucer. We were so popular that we were even invited on a Crimewatch. It was so exciting that I had my fringe cut by a professional hairdresser to look my best. Primrose had gotten the makeup artist to smother her in black eyeliner and lipstick, which got her into serious trouble with her Mum afterwards, but she did not care.

And the highlight of the whole thing? Being awarded the Queen's Police Medal – a rare medal awarded for gallantry or distinguished service. And we were not even in the police force. PC Herman was jealous as sin.

Since then, business has been booming. We are getting more cases than we can handle to be honest. But, as they say, it is better to be busy than quiet, and we now have the luxury of cherry picking the best cases. We are even getting paid for some of them, which is amazing. I am saving up for university, where I am going to study Criminology, and Primrose has nearly enough to buy a Fender Stratocaster guitar, signed by all the members of The Severed Heads.

So, everything should be rosy. It is everything that I thought I ever wanted, but I guess it is like a mountain climber feels once he has reached the summit. What is next? Once you have reached the top, where else is there to go? It is a bittersweet feeling and I have come to realise that like the thrill of the journey is often actually more rewarding than reaching the destination. And what I have come to wonder is, have I already climbed my Everest? At such a young age, have I already peaked? Will I ever get a case as challenging and thrilling as this one ever again? And that worry constantly plagues me.

But then, as these thoughts float around in my head like moths around a light bulb, a letter drops on my doormat. A plain one - nothing fancy. But it is addressed to me. I get a lot of letters now - so many more than I used to. Most of them I throw out. They are usually such trivial matters, such as, which neighbour put their rubbish into my wheelie bin or whose cat keeps pooing in my border of tulips. I know it will probably be in the recycling bin in a few minutes, but every time I open one of these letters, I still get a tingle of anticipation. I am always living in hope. What if it isn't a boring old case? What if it is a big one? What if it is a case to rival the murder at Marden Vale? What if this one is going to be the biggest case of my life?

Printed in Great Britain
by Amazon